Chapter One

I wiped the sweat from my forehead and kept running as fast as I could. I desperately wanted to stop and catch my breath but I didn't have time. I cut straight through the middle of the park, ignoring the signs telling me to keep off the grass. It would take too long to stick to the path winding around the outside. It had been raining over night so the grass was slippy but I refused to slow down. I looked down at my watch and saw that I was already five minutes late. I shouted a combination of my favourite swear words as I watched the seconds tick by.

The next thing I knew, I was on the ground.

Whilst being distracted, I had collided with something hard, bouncing off it and falling backwards on to the wet grass. I looked up, expecting to see a tree or a lamppost but instead stared into a pair of piercing blue eyes. I was instantly transfixed and couldn't bring myself to look away. I shook my head from side to side, feeling disorientated from the fall. I began to wonder if I had hit my head and was just imagining it all. When I was able to process what had actually happened, pure embarrassment took over. There I was, lying flat on my back looking up at the most handsome man that I had ever seen in my whole life. Under normal circumstances, I would be giving myself a big pat on the back right about now.

But not today.

I looked him up and down, taking in the whole package. He was wearing a white shirt with the sleeves rolled up and black skinny jeans, which I had never fully appreciated on a man until this very moment. They fit him to perfection, hugging him in all of the right places. I blushed at the thought and looked back up, noticing his amused expression. I frowned at him as he bit his lip, trying to hide his smile. Well at least somebody found this funny.

He held his hand out to me, "Are you going to stay down there all day?"

His voice was smooth and sexy and I was tempted to take him up on his offer just to hear him speak again. Hell, I was tempted to play dead in the hope that he would give me the kiss of life. Instead, I took his hand and he helped me up in one swift movement.

"Are you okay?" He asked, trying to keep the amusement out of his voice.

"I'm fine. I should have been looking where I was going, sorry."

I watched as his expression changed from being amused to concerned, "Don't be sorry. Are you sure you're not hurt? You took one hell of a fall."

I could feel my cheeks burning as he took hold of my muddy hands and inspected them for any sign of injuries. Now that I was standing up, I could get a better look at him. He was at least six foot tall and looked like he was in his mid-twenties. I could see the outlines of his toned muscles through his shirt and I was pretty sure that he had a six pack hiding under there. His dark brown hair was messy and matched his stubble, giving his good looks a bad boy edge. He looked like a runway model whilst I was a muddy, sweaty mess.

I stopped drooling and realised that he was still holding my hands. He gently brushed his thumb over the inside of my wrist which sent a small shiver through my entire body.

"I'm fine" I blurted out as I quickly took my hands back and bent down to pick up my books. He crouched next to me and handed me my notebook. When I turned to thank him, he was looking at me with one eyebrow raised, "You should really take note of the signs you know." He pointed to one of the annoying 'keep off the grass' signs nearby.

Why are all the good looking guys such douche bags?

"Well so should you" I replied.

"Touché" he said, laughing.

I straightened up and was about to leave when he spoke again, "You can run fast for a girl...you weren't being chased or anything were you?"

I rolled my eyes at him, "Number one, girls can run fast too. Welcome to the 21st century. We're even allowed to vote these days." He feigned shock and I nodded, playing along with him.

2

"Wow, that's a risky move. I see you're allowed to use sarcasm too."

I smiled sweetly, "Number two, no I wasn't being chased and it's a good job or they would have caught up to me by now, thanks to you."

His eyes widened and then he began to nod slowly, "You're right. It's my fault that I was innocently standing here, minding my own business when you tried to rugby tackle me. If it makes you feel any better, I would have protected you from whoever was chasing you."

"Oh wow, that does make me feel better. I'm actually pretty disappointed that I wasn't being chased now, just so I could watch you save me."

I shook my head and looked down at my watch, letting out a big sigh when I saw that I was now ten minutes late. I slung my bag over my shoulder and allowed myself to take one last look at him before walking away.

After taking a few steps, he spoke, "This was nice, we should do it again some time."

I looked over my shoulder and couldn't help but laugh at the handsome smirk on his face.

"Same time tomorrow?" I shouted as I carried on walking.

"It's a date" he shouted back.

I replayed those three little words over and over in my head as I half walked, half jogged the rest of the way to class. Even though I was late to my first ever lecture and was now covered in mud, I couldn't wipe the smile off my face.

I wondered who the beautiful stranger was and more importantly, if he was being serious about the date.

Chapter Two

When I finally arrived at the lecture hall, I was fifteen minutes late. I took a deep breath and was about to go inside when I looked down and saw the mud on my jacket. I took it off and stuffed it into my bag, hoping that the back of my jeans didn't look as bad.

I opened the door and any hint of a smile quickly faded. The Professor stopped talking mid sentence and around two hundred pairs of curious eyes stared back at me. I wanted the ground to open up and swallow me.

I quickly scanned the hall looking for a place to sit. I could feel my cheeks getting redder and redder the longer that I stood there. After what seemed like an eternity, I spotted a seat that only had a bag occupying it. Of course, it was at the very back of the hall right in the middle of a row.

I began my walk of shame, trying not to look anybody in the eye. I could hear a few people whispering as I walked by and one girl rudely tutted in my face. I ignored them and concentrated on not falling over for the second time today. Half way up the stairs, I regretted not working out more and made a mental note to sign up to the local gym.

When I reached the back of the hall, I had to shimmy past everyone in the row to get to the empty seat. I sat down and the boy whose bag had originally been on the seat gave me a warm and sympathetic smile which made me feel a little better.

"Hey" he whispered.

"Hi" I replied.

"I'm Lukas Roberts."

I smiled politely, "April Adams."

"Glad you could make it" he smiled and his warm chocolate brown eyes twinkled down at me. He slid a booklet across the table.

"Thanks," I whispered.

It was an introduction to the course, currently opened at a book list. It was a long list, with thirty or so books on it. Lukas laughed quietly when he saw my shocked expression. I tried to keep a poker face from then on, especially when I found out that the deadline for our first assignment was in just four weeks time. I was relieved that I had chosen to rent a small house on my own, instead of staying in the university halls of residence. At least I would get some peace and quiet to study, even if it meant not having as much money or as much fun as everybody else.

The next forty five minutes went by quickly and before I knew it, everybody was making their way out of the hall. Lukas stood up and packed his books into his bag.

"Thanks for letting me share your booklet, I think you're the only person not mad at me for interrupting."

He smiled and I couldn't help but think how handsome it made him look. He was good looking in a boy next door kind of way. He was about five foot ten with a slim build and sandy blonde hair. He slung his bag over his shoulder.

"Don't worry about it." He spoke with a hint of an accent which I couldn't place.

"Where are you from?" I asked, as we made our way down the stairs.

"Can you not tell?"

I shook my head.

"Well maybe I'll just have to keep talking until you figure it out."

I laughed, "Okay."

"I hope you guess it sooner rather than later though or I'll be talking for a long time. Where are you heading to now?"

"Scotland!" I said, overenthusiastically.

"Why are you going to Scotland?" he asked whilst grinning.

I laughed, "You're from Scotland...well I think that you are anyway..."

"Correct. I grew up in England though, so my accents not as strong as it should be."

By the time we reached the bottom of the stairs, I had almost forgotten about the embarrassing start to the lecture. Almost. Lukas had a calmness about him and I hoped that we were in more classes together.

"Have you got your library induction now?" he asked.

I rolled my eyes, "Yes, because we don't know how a library works by now." He laughed at my clear lack of enthusiasm. "Have you got yours now too?" I asked.

"Yep, I don't have a clue where it is though."

"I do, I ran past it on the way here."

He narrowed his eyes, "You ran here?"

I nodded, "I ran, I fell over, I jogged a bit...the whole shebang."

"You fell over?"

"Did you not wonder why I was covered in mud and grass stains?"

He chucklod, "Yeah but I didn't want to bring it up..."

"Well thank you, I think I've been embarrassed enough for one day. I'm just going to have a quick word with the Professor."

"Is it okay if I wait for you outside and then we can walk to the library together?"

"That sounds good."

I watched as he walked outside before turning my attention to Professor Phillips.

"Professor, can I have a quick word?"

He looked up at me and smiled, "Of course."

"I just want to apologise for being late and interrupting your lecture."

6

"Better late than never. You would probably be surprised at how late some of my students actually turn up. One of my third years has decided to only attend the last ten minutes of my lectures. So in comparison, you were actually early."

I laughed, pleased that I had at least one friendly Professor so far.

"What's your name?" he asked.

"April Adams."

"Welcome to the University of Manchester, April. I hope you enjoy your time here."

I smiled warmly at him, "Thank you, I hope I do too."

I turned and made my way outside, thinking about my morning so far. Although it had been more eventful than I had hoped, I wouldn't change a thing. I smiled, thankful for the warmth of my new class mate, the kindness of my Professor and the mind blowing hotness of the beautiful stranger.

Chapter Three

"I take it back."

"Take what back?" Lukas asked, looking confused.

"The whole...I don't need a library induction. I take it all back."

He laughed, "That makes me feel better, I was starting to worry. I'm never going to find a book that I actually need in this place. Even if I did, I wouldn't know how to loan it out."

"Maybe part of our course is actually finding the books...we might even get credits for it."

"I hope not, I think I'd rather sit more exams" he replied.

I laughed as we carried on following our tour guide and the other students in our group. We walked slowly so that we could talk without getting dirty looks from the over achievers who were frantically scribbling in their notepads. I rolled my eyes, who takes notes during a library induction?

"Maybe we should take notes?" I blurted out, beginning to panic at my lack of enthusiasm.

"You think so?"

"No..." I sighed, "I don't remember any of the libraries back home being this complicated."

"We're not in Kansas anymore" he said.

I tapped my heels together three times whilst chanting, "There's no place like home, there's no place like home, there's no place like home" in my best American accent.

He laughed quietly, "So if you're Dorothy, who does that make me?"

"You're the Scarecrow, obviously."

He frowned, "Are you saying that I don't have a brain?"

"Well it's either that or you've not got a heart...your choice."

"What if I want to be the lion?"

"Okay, you can be the scaredy cat."

He shook his head, "You've only known me for a couple of hours and you're already insulting me...unbelievable."

We both laughed. He was right, for some reason I felt strangely comfortable around him. Maybe it was because he had been kind to me in the lecture whilst everybody else had looked at me like I had just ran over their dog. Lukas was laid back and his chilled out personality reminded me of my friends back home.

I had already lost count of the number of times I wished that my best friend Katie was here with me. We had been inseparable ever since meeting at school and had always planned to be roommates at university. We used to spend hours talking about how much fun we were going to have and about all of the hot, intelligent boys that we were going to meet. When her life had unexpectedly taken her down a different path during our second year of college, I was left to live out our dream alone. I couldn't face sharing a room with a stranger when it should have been Katie, so I decided to rent a small house by myself. It came in handy that I had an older, protective brother who was not only on board with the plan but had agreed to help me out with the rent. It was only small but I loved it. It was a ten minute walk from campus which meant that I was close enough to the hustle and bustle without being too close. Living on my own also meant having a hot shower whenever I wanted.

I looked around the huge library, admiring its beauty and elegance. There were intricate designs painted on the high ceilings and the book cases were made from rich mahogany wood. It was beautiful, even if it wasn't very practical. It made me feel like I was on a movie set rather than inside of a library.

I pointed to a set of rolling library ladders, "They look cool but there's no chance I'm climbing them, I'm not risking my life for a book."

"Now who's the scaredy cat?" he asked whilst grinning.

"I deserved that."

When we caught up to our group, the tour guide was explaining all of the different security measures that were in place to stop students from stealing the books. My first thought was that the criminals around here sounded pretty badass...my second thought was that it had gone from being a library, to a movie set, to an airport.

"It's like an airport with all of this security. I mean, finger print scanners, are they really necessary?"

"Do you think they strip search too?" Lukas asked.

"Only if you're lucky" I pointed to a fat, bald security guard who was walking up and down the aisles holding a walkie talkie.

Before Lukas could respond, a pretty petite girl from our group swivelled around and looked at us with bright green eyes. She was no doubt another goody two shoes about to tell us off for being too loud.

"Did somebody say strip search?" she smiled at Lukas mischievously and ran her fingers through her long black hair.

I looked at Lukas, waiting for him to say something. By the looks of it, we were both caught off guard. When it was obvious that he was just going to ignore her, I answered, "Nope, it wasn't us."

She turned her gaze towards me and narrowed her eyes. After a few seconds, she looked back at Lukas and winked, "It must be my imagination then."

Lukas smiled politely and I was pretty impressed by his ability to resist looking at her cleavage which was proudly on display.

"My names Hollie."

That's funny, I don't remember any of us asking. Meow.

"I'm Lukas and this is April" he replied.

"Is she your girlfriend?"

Wow, straight to the point.

"My girlfriend? No...we're not...I'm...no..." I looked up at him, curious by his flustered response. Hollie was obviously satisfied by his answer and turned to look at me again.

10

"April huh, as in the month?"

"Hollie huh, as in the plant?" I sniped back.

Cue the stupidly high pitched fake laughter. "That's funny but seriously though, were you born in April or something?"

I could tell that she was one of those stereotypical spoilt princesses. She had no doubt been the popular mean girl at school who was both loved and feared by everybody else. I was going to have to bite my tongue around her, I had a tendency to say what was on my mind.

I put on my best fake smile, "Of course I was born in April...April fools day actually. Why else would I be called April? My Mother couldn't think of a name for me so she just called me after the month. I'm just glad that I wasn't born in February or March."

I wasn't going to tell her that my birthday was actually May 27th and that I was named after my late grandmother.

Lukas started coughing to disguise his laughter whilst Hollie looked confused, unsure whether or not to believe me. My bout of sarcasm made my mind wander back to my meeting with the beautiful stranger. Unlike Hollie, he had no problem understanding my sarcasm. He was pretty proficient in it himself, which I liked. I pictured the way that he had looked down at me with his piercing blue eyes and it felt like somebody had turned the heating on full blast. I mentally cursed myself for not finding out who he was.

"Wow, that's pretty lame" Hollie finally announced. I nodded at her, trying to remember what we had even been talking about. Oh yeah, she was being a bitch.

The next thing I knew, the tour guide had stopped talking and was angrily making his way through the group towards us. I was preparing to apologise for talking when Hollie turned around and stopped him in his tracks. It took him all of one second to stare down at her chest. I watched as she bit her lower lip, completely aware of what she was doing.

"I'm sorry, am I being too loud for you?" He was quite clearly speechless and couldn't tear his eyes away from her cleavage. She bent forwards slightly, giving him an even better view, "If you think I'm being loud now, you should hear me in the bedroom." His eyes nearly popped out of his head and he turned beetroot red before scurrying off in the opposite direction, mumbling to himself.

"I guess that means the induction is over, thank god." I had to give it to her, she might be a bitch but she was an old pro at the art of seduction. She turned her attention back to Lukas, "Well it was nice meeting you, I'll definitely be seeing you around." She stroked his chest before walking away.

"Wow..." I said whilst shaking my head.

"I know, I feel kind of violated." He wiped his chest where she had touched him and then looked down at his hands as if they were covered in something disgusting.

I laughed, "I think she's a fan of yours."

He frowned, "I hope not, she's trouble. You can tell from a mile off."

"Trouble? That's a polite way of putting it."

"I know girls like her" he added.

"Well aren't you the lucky one? Now you know one more."

He sighed, "She's obviously used to getting what she wants but that won't be happening with me."

I looked up at him, intrigued by his reaction to Hollie. It was quite refreshing to know that not all men fell for the seductive crap that she had been dishing out.

"Do you want to go for a coffee?" he asked as we made our way out of the library.

"I can't, I've got another class starting in twenty minutes and I don't want to be late."

He smirked, "Well you better get running then."

"Very funny, I've done enough running for one day. See you tomorrow?"

"Wait, are you not going to the mixer tonight?"

"What's a mixer?"

"Oh it's basically just a big party for new students to get to know each other. There's music and a free bar all night. Me and my roommate are going, you should come with us."

"A free bar does sound good but I'm not sure, I don't know anyone."

He laughed, "Well that's kind of the point, you get to meet new people. I can meet you there and we can *mix* together if you want?"

I was pretty tired after my eventful morning and wasn't really in the mood to party but I knew that I should make the effort to get to know new people, especially living off campus.

"Yeah okay, I'm in. Where's it at?"

"It's opposite the Student Union, they're having it outside on the lawn as long as the rain holds off. They set up a portable bar, I've seen photos from last year's."

"Hmmm, I'm trying my best to be optimistic about it being outside. What time shall I meet you?"

"I think we're going around eight. I'll meet you at the bar, do you..." he paused for a moment before continuing, "um...do you want to swap numbers just in case we can't find each other?"

"Sure" I got my phone out and we swapped numbers before I headed off to my next class. I planned on going straight home afterwards and having a hot shower. Then I had the difficult task of planning what to wear for an outdoor party in September.

Luckily, I knew just the right girl for the job.

***

When my class ended, I went home and had a long, hot shower. I stood underneath the water for a long time, until my fingers turned all crinkly. I was grateful to finally stop smelling of wet grass, even if it had secretly been a nice little reminder of my meeting with the beautiful stranger.

Wrapped only in a towel and my hair still dripping down my back, I rang Katie and told her all about my first day. She laughed for a whole minute straight when I told her about falling over but she quickly turned all serious when I told her how it had happened. As expected, she wanted to hear every little detail and told me off for not asking for his name or number. She practically begged me to go back tomorrow but I told her that he must have been joking about the date. I would feel like a loser if I went back and he didn't show up. By the time we stopped talking about him, my hair was completely dry. I quickly filled her in on the rest of my day including Lukas and my encounter with Hollie.

"It's a good job I wasn't there, I would have wiped that smug smile straight off her face."

I laughed "I know but I still wish that you were here."

She sighed down the phone, "Me too. I'm sorry, A."

"Don't be silly, you've got more important things going on in your life. You're blessed to have a husband and a healthy baby boy who will love you forever, even when you're old and wrinkly."

"They better had do, I had two hours sleep last night...two hours!"

"You should be used to it after all of our partying."

"Nothing can prepare you for this, it's exhausting. Just you wait..."

"Oh don't you worry, I intend on waiting a very long time."

"Well thanks for letting me in on that plan. Anyway, what are you going to wear tonight for this garden thingy?"

"Well that's where you need to help me...I don't have a clue."

"Why are they having it outside?"

"Because they're idiots, hot blooded ones apparently."

"I guess you won't even notice after all of the drinking and dancing."

14

"Unless it rains..."

"Well take an umbrella just in case. I think the safe bet is to wear jeans and a cute top."

"What kinds of shoes?"

"Heels, of course."

"Heels and grass don't mix."

"Well you said the same thing about me and Ian, now look where we are..."

Katie had met Ian whilst we were in our second year of college and fell pregnant after dating him for three months. It was a big shock for both of us and she spent many nights sobbing round at my house. Ian took the news surprisingly well and actually proposed to her. She said no initially because she thought that he was asking her for the wrong reasons. They eventually got married last month. I was her maid of honour and carried their son Jamie down the aisle.

"Point taken. I'll wear heels but if I get stuck in the mud, I'm blaming you. Thanks for listening to me ramble on, I'll let you go do mummy stuff."

"Okay, have fun tonight. Make sure you dance with lots of cute guys for me. Ring me tomorrow to give me all of the gossip."

"Will do, miss you."

"Miss you too."

After hanging up, I put some upbeat music on to stop me from getting upset. I missed my friends back home but I was going to have to suck it up and adjust to my new life here. I poured myself a glass of wine and sipped it whilst I did my hair and make-up. Then it was time to find an outfit.

After trying on nearly half of my wardrobe, I decided to wear my dark blue skinny jeans and a red silk and lace top which showed just the right amount of skin. I put on my black peep toe shoes and matching leather jacket.

Although my house was only ten minutes away from the university, I didn't want to walk in my heels so I rang up for a taxi. I text Lukas whilst I was waiting to tell him that I would be there soon.

When the taxi arrived, I checked myself in the mirror one last time before heading out.

Show time.

Chapter Four

I took a deep breath as I stepped out of the taxi. There were easily a few hundred people on the lawn. The mixer was in full force and it was blatantly obvious that a lot of people were already drunk. The music was blaring and the drinks were flowing. I was impressed at the set up, especially the portable bar. It looked like one that you would see in a swanky night club, with lights overhead and stools to sit on. There were outdoor sofas and bean bags scattered around a tiled area acting as a dance floor. At least my heels might not get ruined after all. It looked completely different from this afternoon. I panicked a little, wondering how I was going to find Lukas but then I remembered that I could just call him.

I cautiously made my way over to the bar, ignoring a few sleazy looks that I got along the way. I stood in the queue waiting to be served when I noticed a group of very loud girls who were wearing very little stood at the opposite end of the bar. They were all gathered around a man and were doing their best to out-flirt and out-giggle one another. I rolled my eyes at their desperate need for attention.

As if he could read my mind, the man turned around and looked straight at me. My heart almost leapt out of my chest. It was the beautiful stranger from this morning, looking even more beautiful than I remembered. It felt like the world stopped turning and all that mattered in that moment was our connection. His eyes burned into mine. His fan club must have noticed that his attention was elsewhere as they started looking in my direction too. I looked away as I didn't want a group of bitchy Barbie Dolls on my back.

I hovered at the bar, waiting to be served whilst my mind was racing. God, he was so gorgeous. I peeked over my shoulder to see if he was still there but both him and his fan club were gone.

"Looking for me?" a voice whispered in my ear, making me jump. I turned around to see the beautiful stranger smiling down at me. His closeness sent a rush of excitement through my whole body. I took a deep breath, trying to calm my nerves.

"Are you stalking me?" I replied.

"Do I look like a stalker?"

I raised an eyebrow, "Do you really want me to answer that?"

He grinned, "Well I can tell that you've missed me."

"Yep, like a hole in the head."

Liar.

"You're way too sweet, it's actually pretty sickly. You should work on toning it down a notch or two before somebody throws up on you."

I thought I heard him say something about being sick but my mind was preoccupied. All I could concentrate on was how incredibly sexy he looked in a suit. If I thought that he was handsome this morning then he was taking it to a whole new level right now. I was pretty sure that if I got my hands on some GQ magazines, I would find him on several of the front covers.

His hair was still messy which drove me crazy as it looked like he had just gotten out of bed. I began to wonder what his bedroom would look like and what I would look like in it. I blushed at the thought, I'd never been any good at hiding my emotions. I noticed that his stubble had gone which made me want to reach out and touch his smooth, chiselled face. He looked at me with the same amused expression that he had worn this morning. It took my breath away and I mentally cursed myself for being so easily affected by him.

He looked down at his expensive looking watch, who knew that watches could be sexy? "You're late...again."

"For what?" I asked.

"I've been waiting for you."

I narrowed my eyes, "But you didn't even know that I was coming."

"I'm a stalker, remember? You said it yourself. We know these things." He winked at me and I tried my best not to grin like a total idiot.

"Can I get you a drink?" he asked.

I cocked my head to the side, "It's a free bar..."

"I know but I can't see a drink in front of you."

I shrugged, "The service is slow."

"What do you want?"

You.

Thank god I didn't blurt out the first thing that popped into my head.

"Red wine, please."

Without saying another word, he leant over the bar and motioned to one of the bar staff. A pretty girl with fire red hair rushed over and fluttered her eye lashes at him. It didn't take long to realise that I wasn't the only one affected by him. After ignoring me completely, she served him our drinks. He thanked her before handing me the glass of wine.

"I could have got my own but thanks."

"When? Next year?" he asked.

Jerk.

I watched him sip his orange juice, "Do you not drink?" I asked.

"I do, but not tonight."

"Oh, are you driving?"

"Nope."

I wondered why he wasn't drinking, especially when it was a free bar but I didn't press him for an answer.

"Do you want to sit down?" he asked.

I looked around and couldn't see Lukas anywhere, "Okay." He led me over to one of the leather sofas. I was glad that I had decided to wear jeans and not a skirt.

"You look lovely this evening" he said as he sat down next to me.

"Thanks" I replied, trying to stop myself from blushing like a school girl.

"I'm a little disappointed that you're not falling at my feet again though. Has the novelty worn off now?"

I rolled my eyes and he laughed.

"So what do you want to do on our date tomorrow?"

I looked at him wide eyed, trying to judge whether he was being serious. "Don't tell me that you've forgotten about it already?" he asked.

"I've not forgotten…"

"Good. So do you want to go somewhere in particular or just roll around on the floor again? Personally, I'm leaning towards the latter." He raised his eyebrow suggestively which set my whole body on fire. I was tempted to answer honestly but my self-preservation kicked in.

"I did not roll around on the floor."

"Well you were down there for a pretty long time."

"I was dazed, I ran straight into your freakishly hard body remember?"

He smirked, "How could I forget? It's not every day that I have a beautiful woman pressed up against me."

Deep breaths. In through your nose, out through your mouth.

"What were you doing lurking in the park anyway?" I asked.

"I'll show you if you want."

"When?" I asked a little too fast.

He laughed, "Whenever you want. We could go now, if you'd like?"

I thought about it for a moment. It would be pretty damn stupid of me to wander off into the night with a complete stranger…a completely beautiful stranger.

"Okay."

His face turned serious as he leaned in closer, "I need you to promise me that in future you will never take off with somebody who you've only just met...it could get you hurt." I could see the concern in his eyes which made me question what I was about to do. Call me crazy but my instincts were telling me that I could trust him.

"Well what about you?" I asked.

A small smile crept across his face, "I'm the only exception."

I laughed, "Of course you are."

"Do you promise?"

I nodded at him, feeling strangely happy that this beautiful man was concerned about my personal safety.

"Say it."

Well hello there, Mr Bossy.

"I promise."

"Good, now follow me."

He led us into the park. The lights from the party grew dim and the music grew quiet. The grass was still damp...so much for not getting my heels dirty. I walked slowly and carefully, making sure that I didn't fall over in front of him again. It caught me off guard when he grabbed hold of my hand and placed it on his bicep, "Hold on, I won't let you fall."

My heart started beating so hard that I thought it was going to hammer its way out of my chest. "Thanks," I managed to mutter. Screw walking, all I could concentrate on was the feel of his muscle. My knees nearly gave way when I felt it tense up.

"Who are you here with tonight? I don't want them worrying about you" he asked.

"Nobody. I was meant to be meeting someone but I couldn't see them anywhere. What about you?"

"I'm on my own."

"It didn't look like you were on your own when I arrived." I struggled to keep the bitterness out of my voice and he looked pleased at my reaction.

"You've got nothing to be jealous of."

I scoffed, "I'm not jealous."

Liar.

"I'm pretty sure that no one else could roll around in mud and still look breathtakingly beautiful."

I looked up at him expecting him to be joking but he was dead serious. The blue of his eyes shone bright in the darkness. Did he actually just call me beautiful? Maybe I should fall over more often. I cleared my throat, "I didn't roll around in it..."

He laughed, "You're so easy to wind up, its adorable."

Beautiful and adorable? I can't take much more.

The park was eerily quiet but I didn't feel afraid. I felt safe holding on to this beautiful stranger whose name I didn't even know. I knew that I was acting pretty reckless but I didn't care.

His walking slowed until we came to a stop. "Recognise this place?" he asked. I glanced around and realised that it was the spot where I had fallen over this morning. He gave me the most perfect smile and I had to grip on to him a little tighter.

"It's where we met and where I fell over like a complete idiot" I answered.

"You're not an idiot, sometimes it's impossible to stop ourselves from falling." He winked before swooping me up into his arms. Of course, I did what any person would do when they were trying to impress a sex god...I squealed like a big girl.

"What are you doing? Put me down!" I wriggled, trying to get free.

"Stop wriggling, this is for your own good. As much as I would love to see you on your knees, I'm pretty sure that you don't want to fall over again."

I died. I died in his arms and went straight to heaven. I stopped wriggling and instead focused on how close he was holding me to him. His chest was warm and I was pretty sure that I could feel his heart beating.

He smiled down at me, "That's better. See, you can be a good girl."

The way he said it made it sound so erotic that I had to close my eyes and compose myself before I did something crazy. I didn't feel like being a good girl right now.

When I opened my eyes, I could see something twinkling up ahead, "What's that?" I asked.

"You'll see."

We carried on walking until we reached a small clearing with a large oak tree in the centre. It had lanterns hanging from its branches which gave it a kind of magical feel. It looked like something out of a movie. He carefully placed me down underneath it so that my back was leaning against the trunk. He sat down next to me, "So...what do you think?"

"I'm speechless."

"That must be a first for you."

"Speaking of firsts, when are you going to stop being a jerk?"

A devilish grin appeared on his face.

"So what is it?" I asked, looking around.

"It's a tree."

"Well yeah, but what's with all of the lanterns?"

He shrugged and looked around, "It's dark."

I smiled at his sarcasm, it was quickly becoming one of my favourite things about him. "Did you set this up?" I asked.

"Yep, do you like it?"

I nodded and answered honestly, "Yeah, it's pretty...it's also a little bit weird."

He laughed, "Weird how?"

"It just is. We're in the middle of a secluded park. What's with all of the lanterns? Is this some kind of special tree?"

He smiled, "I come here to write, sometimes at night. I like this place, it's peaceful."

"So you're a writer?"

He nodded.

"What do you write?"

"Songs, usually. I've written novels too, it depends what mood I'm in."

"Are you going to write something tonight?"

"I could do, I happen to have a lot of inspiration right now." He raised one eyebrow, "But to be honest, I'm not really in the mood to write..."

As much as my head was telling me to look away from him, I couldn't. It was like some kind of magnetic force, keeping our eyes fixed on each other. "What are you in the mood for?" I asked.

"Trust me, you don't want to know."

It's official, I'm screwed.

"Trust me, I do" I replied, feeling brave.

"But I don't want to scare you off already."

"Do your worst."

He leant in so that our faces were almost touching. I could feel the warmth of his breath as I watched his every move. His eyes were fixed on my mouth and it was only then that I realised I was holding my breath. He slowly brought his hand up to my face and brushed his thumb over my lips. He lifted his eyes back up to meet mine, just as the sound of a girl laughing made me jump.

He quickly moved his hand away and stood up before helping me up. I looked around and spotted a boy and girl walking in our direction. They were kissing and teasing each other. Their motive for coming into the park was pretty obvious and I panicked in case they thought the same of me. As they got closer, I heard the girl point out the lanterns to the boy and then waited for them to notice that they weren't alone.

The girl fell silent and looked down at the floor when she noticed us. The boy grinned, "Sorry, man. I didn't know anybody else was out here."

"No problem" my beautiful stranger replied, placing his hands in his trouser pockets.

"Nice set up" the boy said as he grabbed hold of the girls hand and carried on walking.

We both stayed silent until I couldn't bear it anymore, "Do you think he's going to show her his lanterns?"

He raised an eyebrow and laughed, "Definitely. She seemed a little overwhelmed by mine."

I shook my head but couldn't keep the grin off my face, "I've seen bigger..."

"Now you're just trying to make me jealous."

"Have you got lantern envy?"

"Yes, I hope you're pleased with yourself."

I laughed, "I am."

He sat back down and I joined him, "So is that what you were doing here this morning, writing?"

"Yep, I was heading home when you ran into me...literally."

"Yes I know, I was there remember? So when did you light the candles?"

"When I got here tonight, before everybody started to arrive."

"So you must have been planning on coming out here at some point..."

He shrugged, "I knew that I was going to need some quiet time sooner or later. Sometimes it can get a little too much with all the students, especially when they're drinking, you know?"

I nodded. I was eager to learn more about this beautiful man. He was intriguing and different from anybody else that I had ever met. Not to mention, hotter than hot.

I could see him looking at me out of the corner of my eye. I looked down at my jeans, fiddling with a loose piece of cotton and when I looked back up, he was still looking at me. "What?" I asked him.

"Sorry, it's just that I'm not used to other people being here with me, it's nice. I've never shown anybody this place, you're my first" he smirked at me.

I rolled my eyes, "I bet you say that to all the girls."

"So is that why you're playing hard to get? Because you think that I'm some kind of ladies man?"

"I'm not playing anything," I said defensively.

He chuckled, "Okay..."

"I'm not!" I protested, frustrated at his disbelieving tone. "Which part of me walking into the woods alone with you at night is playing hard to get?"

He grinned and held his hands up, "Okay, okay...no games." He waited a few moments before speaking again, "So I've got to ask, what are your thoughts on role playing then?"

I shook my head whilst he laughed at me. "You know, all of this is pretty weird" I said.

"Is that so?"

"Yes, I'm sat under a tree in the middle of the night with some guy whose name I don't even know."

He raised his eyebrows, "Some guy huh? Is that how you see me?"

"Well you're a guy and I don't know your name, so yes."

"Well you've not asked me what my name is. Plus it's a two way street, I don't know yours either."

"Well you've not asked me...two way street remember?"

"Okay. My name's Isaac, I'm twenty four, I play the piano and my favourite colour is red," he glanced down at my red top and then up to my red lips. "Your lipstick is driving me fucking crazy."

Subconsciously, I licked my lips at the mention of it. My heart started to beat stupidly fast when I saw the fire ignite in his eyes. After a moment, he spoke again, "There, now you know all of the important stuff. It's a pleasure to meet you."

For some reason, now that I knew his name, the connection between us felt more real. I nodded but was occupied by thoughts of him playing the piano...shirtless.

What a pervert.

"This is usually the part where you tell me your name..."

"April" It came out as a whisper.

"April." I loved the way my name sounded coming out of his mouth. I could listen to him saying it all day or all night long. "What a beautiful name, it suits you."

"It should do, it's been my name for twenty years."

"Wow, you'll be collecting your pension soon" he said, sarcastically.

"No that's you, Granddad. It's okay, it's common for people to get confused in their old age."

"I'm like a fine wine, I get better with age."

I laughed at his analogy, "Do you get better at being arrogant too?"

"I'm not arrogant...I'm just amazing" he grinned from ear to ear and I couldn't help but smile. The pathetic thing was, I actually agreed with him but I wasn't about to make his head even bigger.

"You do know that I'm only joking, right?" he asked.

"I *hope* that you're only joking."

"I am, I don't want you thinking that I'm some arrogant jerk."

"I don't think that you're arrogant..."

He laughed and bumped his shoulder into mine. I got excited by the contact. A little bit of shoulder contact and he sends my head spinning. Lord knows what I'd be like if we had any other type of contact.

"Well I'll prove to you that I'm not a jerk, we've got plenty of time for that. Speaking of which, what would you like to do tomorrow?"

"So it's a real date then?" I asked.

"As opposed to what? A fake date?"

"I didn't know if you were joking."

"Hell no, this is all very real. There's no backing out."

I grinned, wondering what on earth I had done to make this gorgeous man want to take me out on a date. Maybe falling over was the way forward.

"I won't back out. What time are you thinking? I've got classes all day."

"I'm busy in the day too. I'll pick you up around seven and take you to dinner, I know a really nice Italian restaurant."

"Sounds good" I said whilst grinning like an idiot.

He reached into his jacket pocket and took out his mobile, "Let's swap numbers, you can text me your address."

I got my phone out of my bag, trying to stay calm and not freak out like a loser. It was all becoming very real, very quickly. After reading his number out to me, I saved it and dropped it back into my bag.

He sat and stared at me with his phone in his hand, "Are you not going to give me yours?"

Back home, I had been used to taking phone numbers but not giving mine out that it had been an automatic response. "I'll think about it." I laughed at his shocked expression.

"I thought you said that you weren't playing games."

I pouted at him and watched as his gaze turned heated. He pulled at his shirt collar and loosened his tie, "I think I should get you back to the party."

I felt disappointment flood through me, I could quite happily sit here and talk to him all night. It must have shown on my face as he laughed and raised his eyebrow, "It's for your own good, trust me."

"I think I should be the judge of that."

His eyes widened as he bit his bottom lip. "Oh really?" he asked as he leant in closer to me. I nodded, my heart beating at record speed. I was convinced that he would be able to hear it. He pulled away with a wicked grin on his face, "I'll make sure you have plenty of things to judge me on tomorrow night. But right now we better get back, I don't want your friends worrying about you."

I had completely forgotten that I was supposed to be meeting Lukas, "I don't even know if he's here yet, he's not rang me."

Isaac frowned, "He?"

"Um...yeah..."

"Who is *he*?"

"Just a guy off my course."

"Does *he* have a name?"

"Of course *he* has a name, it's Lukas."

"Did you meet him today?"

Jeez, he was even sexier when he was being moody.

I grinned, "You've got nothing to be jealous of..."

He smiled, his face relaxing a little. "Was tonight meant to be a date?"

"No," I answered a little too quickly.

He looked pleased at my answer, "Good. Although I must say, I'm a little upset that you've given this Lukas guy your number but you won't give it to me."

If only you knew what I would give you.

"Well he didn't knock me over this morning and make me late for class."

He stood up and grinned down at me, "Don't act like it wasn't the highlight of your day."

I ignored the hand that he held out for me and stood up by myself, "The highlight of my day? Don't you mean the highlight of my *year*?" I said, sarcastically.

"Well obviously. I just wanted to hear the words coming out of your mouth."

I rolled my eyes, "Well thanks for showing me your tree anyway."

"I'll show you my tree any time." I couldn't help but laugh at how dirty he made it sound.

"What about your lanterns?" I asked.

"They're a package deal."

I loved that we had the same sense of humour. I went to hold on to his arm again but he took my hand and held it tightly in his. I looked up at him questioningly but he just smiled. I thought that it would have felt strange holding somebody's hand when I hardly knew them but it didn't. He wasn't just somebody.

As we got closer to the party, the music grew louder and a slower song that I recognised began to play. He stopped at the edge of the park, where we were still concealed by a line of trees. "Would you care to dance?" he asked.

"What? Here?"

"It's a little less crowded than the dance floor."

I smiled up at him, "I would love to dance."

I placed my hands around his neck and got chills when I felt his fingers caress the small of my back. I looked into his eyes and was suddenly overwhelmed by our connection. There was an electricity in the air and I knew that he felt it too. He was a good mover, spinning and dipping me in all of the right places. By the end of the song, I didn't want it to end. He leant down and whispered thank you in my ear before softly pressing his lips against my neck. I gasped as it sent tingles through my entire body. I desperately wanted to turn my head and kiss him whilst running my hands through his messed up hair. He evoked something inside of me that I had never felt before. He looked at me as if he was waiting for my reaction.

"I think I should dance with you more often if that's how you're going to thank me" I whispered.

His eyes sparkled, "In that case, I'll take you dancing tomorrow night."

"Deal."

We carried on walking until we rejoined the party. He didn't take my hand this time, it wouldn't look very innocent walking out of the park together hand in hand. We walked over to the bar and I lost count of the number of drunk people we walked past. One girl was bent over being sick whilst several idiots ogled her backside.

"I see what you mean about it getting a bit too much" I said. He laughed and nodded.

I wasn't surprised to see a fair number of people wave at Isaac and say hello to him. I guessed that he would be pretty popular around campus, especially with the girls.

When we got to the bar, I looked around for Lukas.

"Can you see him?" Isaac asked. I could hear the bitterness in his voice.

"Nope."

"Good job I was here then."

"Yep, just like it was a good job that you were in the park this morning. You know, to save me from anybody who might have been chasing me."

I felt a tap on my shoulder and spun around.

"Lukas, hey."

"Hey April, I'm really sorry I'm late. My phone battery died so I couldn't call you. Have you been waiting long?"

"No, don't worry about it."

Isaac coughed.

"Lukas this is Isaac. Isaac, Lukas."

Lukas smiled and extended his hand, "Hey."

"Nice to meet you" Isaac replied as they shook hands.

Lukas turned to look over his shoulder, "This is my roommate, Dan." Dan raised his hand up in greeting and I smiled back at him.

The other people at the bar were becoming a little rowdy. Isaac looked at me with a concerned expression, "Do you want to sit down? There's a couch free over there."

Lukas looked at the couch and then back to me, "Yeah you should go and sit down, I'll bring you a drink over. What would you like?"

"Thanks, red wine please."

"Red wine coming up."

"I thought that it was a free bar?" Isaac teased as he led me over to the couch.

"Do you want me to go back and get my own drink?"

"I wouldn't let you even if you tried."

I looked over my shoulder and saw Dan saying something to Lukas whilst watching us. I think they had expected Isaac to stay with them but I was glad that he hadn't.

"Are you trying to get me alone again?" I teased as I sat down.

"Can you blame me? I don't like sharing."

God, it was hot outside tonight or maybe it was just the fire in his eyes.

"I've never been good at sharing" I admitted.

"If you were mine, you would never have to share."

I felt like I was going to explode, I couldn't remember the last time that I had felt like this.

He looked over at the bar, where Lukas was now being served, "I'm going to be honest with you. I don't want to sit here all night making small talk when all I want to do is kiss you."

"Well I don't want to sit here all night making small talk *knowing* that all you want to do is kiss me."

"Then don't."

When my eyes wandered over to Lukas, he sighed, "What am I going to do with you?"

"I can think of a few things..."

"Oh really?"

I nodded and he grinned, "I'd like to hear some of your suggestions tomorrow."

"Deal."

I was already excited to see him again and he hadn't even left yet. I watched as he stood up, "Are you going to be okay here or do you want me to take you home?"

"I want you to take me home...but I'll be okay here" I replied.

I could see the twinkle in his eye as he grinned down at me, "Well don't have too much fun without me. Text me when you get home or I won't be able to sleep."

I grinned, "Maybe I want to keep you up all night."

"I don't doubt that for a second. Good night beautiful."

I melted at hearing him call me beautiful for the second time this evening. It was something that I could easily get used to.

"Sweet dreams," I replied as I smiled up at him.

"Oh I will" he grinned at me before walking backwards, never taking his eyes away from mine. After taking a few more steps, he bumped into some guy and nearly sent his drink flying. I tried my best not to laugh. His gaze finally left mine as he turned around to apologise to him.

I could see Lukas and Dan on their way over to me with our drinks so I took one last glance at Isaac. Luckily, the guy who he had bumped into was now laughing and for some reason, looking straight at me. I was embarrassed and could feel the heat rising in my cheeks when Isaac pointed at me. However, embarrassment was quickly replaced with a completely different emotion all together when I heard him say the words that I knew I was never going to forget, "I'm going to marry that girl one day."

And in that moment...I knew that I was falling in love.

***

I stayed at the party for another hour after Isaac had left, chatting and dancing with Lukas and Dan. I got talking to some other people off our course which made me feel a lot more positive about spending the next three years here without my friends from back home. Although I enjoyed being around Lukas, I couldn't stop thinking about Isaac. I got butterflies when I thought about the last thing that he had said before leaving. Did he really mean it? How could he possibly know something like that? One thing was for sure, I wanted to find out. My feelings for him were overwhelming and I just wanted to fast forward time until I got to see him again. I kept picturing the way he looked at me with his piercing blue eyes and the way he bit his bottom lip. I was surprised that nobody asked me why I kept randomly blushing.

Dan ended up going back to some drunk girls house so me and Lukas shared a taxi home. On the way back, we talked about our similar taste in music and sports and I was glad that he hadn't ditched me to go with Dan. He refused to let me pay my share of the taxi fare and waited until I got into my house and locked the door before leaving. I was thankful to have met somebody like him and I knew that we were going to be good friends.

After taking my clothes and make up off, I climbed into bed just after midnight. With Isaac still on my mind, I typed him a quick text message -

"Just got in bed. Get some sleep. April x"

He replied almost instantly -

"Glad you're home safe, wish I was there to tuck you in."

I grinned like a Cheshire cat as I typed my message back to him -

"Another time? x"

Within seconds, his name was flashing across my screen -

"Later today is another time."

I got lightheaded when I thought about spending time alone with him.

Before falling asleep, I decided to send Katie a quick message -

"Sorry if this wakes you up. Tonight was amazing! Guess who was there? My mystery man from the park!! We're going on a date tomorrow, eeeek!! xx"

I laughed when I read her reply -

"I NEED DETAILS!! RING ME TOMORROW!! X"

I placed my phone on my bedside table and fell asleep almost instantly. I dreamt that I was sitting under the candle lit tree with Isaac. Only this time, we didn't rejoin the party.

I was never going to be able to look at a tree in the same way again.

Chapter Five

I woke up the next morning with a stupid grin plastered on my face. It was hard to believe that just twenty four hours ago, Isaac didn't even exist in my world. I was so thankful that I had been running late yesterday and that Lukas persuaded me to go to the mixer. I may never have met him otherwise.

I practically skipped to the shower and then sang at the top of my lungs for the next twenty minutes. Whilst getting dressed, I heard the familiar sound of a new text message. I crossed my fingers, hoping that it was Isaac. I squealed when I saw his name on the screen.

"Morning beautiful. Sleep well?"

My cheeks were beginning to ache from smiling so much.

"Very well actually. I had some interesting dreams..."

I blushed as I hit the send button. Within seconds he replied -

"Can't wait to hear all about them tonight. Don't forget to send me your address."

I did as he asked and then finished getting ready, my thoughts consumed with images of him.

On my walk over to class, I decided to try and put him out of my mind for the next few hours. It was only my second day and I needed to concentrate properly. Thinking about Isaac would definitely distract me from my work.

When I got to my first lecture of the day, I was glad to see a few people that I recognised from the mixer. I waved to a girl called Lucy and said hello to a couple of other people as I made my way over to Lukas. Today's entrance definitely beat yesterday's.

"Hey, I saved you a seat" Lukas said, smiling up at me.

"Which one?" I laughed as I looked at the available seats at either side of him.

"Take your pick."

I chose the seat closest to me before taking my notebook out of my bag.

"Did you have fun last night?" he asked.

"Yeah it was awesome, I'm really glad that I went."

So much for not thinking about Isaac. Banishing him from my thoughts was going to be harder than I'd hoped.

"Thanks for making sure that I got home safe" I added.

"No problem. I really enjoyed it too, although I didn't enjoy listening to Dan throwing up all morning."

I tried not to laugh, "Bad times. At least he made it home."

"Is that supposed to be a good thing? I'd rather him stay out all night. I don't know what was worse, listening to him throw up or listening to him replay the events of last night in sordid detail."

A boy who was sat in front of us turned around and smirked. I rolled my eyes but before I could say anything, the Professor announced that the lecture was about to start.

The next hour went by quickly and I didn't have the chance to think about anything other than what the Professor was saying. It helped that the topic was interesting, I was fascinated by anything to do with the brain and cognition. But I was pretty sure that I wouldn't be so lucky in my next lecture. I looked down at my scribbled notes and didn't have a clue how I was going to read them after today. I packed my things into my bag and made my way outside with Lukas.

"I've learnt something new about you" he said.

"What's that?"

"You can write super fast, I saw smoke coming off your notebook at one point."

I laughed, "Maybe, but what use is it if I can't read it afterwards?"

"True, it did look like something out of the Da Vinci Code. So what lecture have you got next?"

I sighed, "Research methods, I'm going to fall asleep. What about you?"

"Group work and communication skills, equally as entertaining."

"Well aren't we the enthusiasts? It's only day two." I shook my head and we both laughed.

"Do you want to meet up for coffee afterwards? We might need it to wake us up" he asked.

"I swear that I'm not just avoiding having coffee with you but I can't. I've got my tutor meeting straight after my lecture."

"No problem. Who's your tutor? Maybe they can help decode your lecture notes."

"How come I never thought of that? I can't remember his name, it's over in the Synergy building. Who's yours?"

"Professor Phillips, I had my meeting with him yesterday."

"He seems really friendly. What do personal tutors actually do?"

"Mainly admin stuff. They basically monitor our progress throughout the year and check that we're not having any problems or falling behind in classes. They can provide us with things like references and work placements."

"References? Maybe I should take him an apple, try to sweeten him up a little bit."

"I like apples," he held his hands up, "just saying..."

I laughed, "I'll try to remember that. Are you in the law lecture this afternoon?"

"Yep, I'll save you a seat."

"What if I get there first?"

"Then you can save me one." He looked at me like I had just asked him a trick question.

"I see how it is, I was late one time and now you've stereotyped me." I laughed and waved to him before walking to my next lecture.

***

To my surprise, it wasn't half as boring as I thought it was going to be. I sat next to Lucy, the girl who I had met at the mixer last night. She had a pretty bad hangover which made me proud of myself for not getting in a similar state.

After the lecture, I walked straight to the Synergy building for my tutor meeting. I happily listened to my iPod and ate a granola bar on the way. I arrived in plenty of time and looked for the signs to room 316. I considered taking the stairs for all of two seconds before waiting for the lift, my excuse was that I wanted to be fresh for the meeting.

I got out on the third floor and began to look at the room numbers on the doors. I was heading in the right direction when I noticed Hollie waiting outside one of the rooms. After our meeting in the library yesterday, she wasn't exactly on my Christmas card list. My plan was to walk past and pretend that I didn't see her but it was too late, she had already spotted me. She looked me up and down before plastering on a fake smile.

"No boyfriend today?" she asked in her stupidly high pitched voice. At first I was confused by her comment but then I realised that she must have been talking about Lukas.

"He's not my boyfriend."

She gave me a sympathetic look, "Don't worry, I'm sure someone will go out with you one day."

What a bitch.

"Thank you, I'll be able to sleep tonight knowing that." I shook my head at her and carried on walking down the corridor, keeping my eye on the room numbers. I got right to the end and still hadn't found room 316.

That's when it hit me like a ton of bricks. I groaned out loud when I realised that it must have been the one that Hollie was standing outside of. I took a deep breath and began to walk back in her direction.

She smirked, "Nice walk?"

I ignored her and instead looked at the shiny door plate behind her.

316.

Awesome.

"Are you here for your tutor meeting?" she asked.

I nodded and then leant against the wall on the opposite side of her. I put my earphones in, wondering why on earth I had to have the same personal tutor as Hollie. I hoped that the meetings were going to be separate so I wouldn't have to spend any more time with her. She mouthed something to me but I just shook my head and pointed to my earphones.

Five minutes later, the door to 316 opened and I got a very pleasant surprise. My heart leapt out of my chest when I saw Isaac standing in front of me. I was ridiculously attracted to him, he looked better each time I saw him.

All of the memories from last night came flooding back as a huge smile crept across my face. I pulled my earphones out and was about to ask what he was doing here when I noticed the look on his face. He wasn't smiling. I could feel the tension in the air immediately. I knew that something wasn't right but I was too afraid to say anything. We stayed silent and stared at each other as the seconds felt like minutes.

"Can I go inside?" I jumped when Hollie spoke, forgetting that she was even there.

I glanced at her and she looked suspicious. Her eyes were narrowed and she was looking back and forth between me and Isaac.

He cleared his throat, "Yes, of course. Please go in." Why did she ask Isaac if she could go inside? My mind didn't seem to be working fast enough.

Isaac waited until Hollie went inside before taking a step

towards me, "I'm sorry, I swear I didn't know."

Know what? I looked at the open door and then back to him trying to understand what was happening. I took a step to the side and looked into the room where Hollie was now sitting down. She was the only person in there. I felt sick when the penny finally dropped. I desperately wanted to believe that it wasn't true and that I had come to the wrong conclusion.

"No...you can't be" I whispered. I could see the disappointment in his eyes. "You're my..." I couldn't bear to say it. He closed his eyes and nodded, confirming my fears. I felt completely blindsided and embarrassed as I remembered some of the inappropriate things that I had said to him.

Jesus, what if we would have taken things further? Although we had only met yesterday, our connection was undeniable. Last night was one of the best nights of my life and who knew what might have happened on our date tonight. I felt stupid. Stupid for letting myself have such strong feelings for somebody that I hardly knew. Stupid for not asking more questions last night. Stupid for believing that I was falling in love with my goddamn tutor.

"Why didn't you tell me?" I asked.

"I didn't know" he whispered as he took hold of my hand and led us down the corridor, away from his office. After a while, I stopped and let go of his hand.

"But you knew that I was a student and you were a member of staff. You should have told me." I could feel myself starting to get angry and began to question his motives.

"You're right, it was wrong of me not to tell you straight away but..."

"Do you hit on all of your students?" I regretted saying it as soon as the words left my mouth. I knew in my heart that he wasn't that kind of person but the damage had been done.

"How could you even think that?" I could see the hurt in his eyes and couldn't bear to look at him any longer. I was feeling too many emotions all at once. I walked away from him and wanted to go home but I didn't have a clue who I would need to see about swapping tutors. Plus, I would have to come up with an excuse for why I wanted to swap which might look suspicious.

I stopped outside his office and took a deep breath before going inside. I copied Hollie and put on a fake smile before sitting down in the chair next to her. She looked at me questioningly, "What was all that about?"

"Nothing" I replied.

"It didn't look like nothing." I knew that she wasn't going to let it drop.

I sighed, "I spilt a drink on him at the mixer last night, I was pretty wasted. I didn't know he was my tutor until now so as you can imagine, I'm a little embarrassed. I've just apologised to him." If only that was the truth, it would be so much easier to deal with. Maybe then I wouldn't have to sit here feeling like I was going to burst into tears.

"Wow, how embarrassing. It's even worse because he's so freaking hot."

My blood boiled when she called him hot but at least she seemed to buy my excuse.

My stomach did a somersault when Isaac walked into the room. By the look on his face, I could tell that this was difficult for him too. I could feel the tension radiating off both of us. I glanced at Hollie and was glad that she didn't seem to notice. She was concentrating on using her cleavage to get his attention.

Isaac sat down behind his desk and put a pair of black, thick rimmed glasses on. I should have guessed that he would look even hotter wearing glasses. He seriously had to be the hottest tutor in the history of hot tutors. I wasn't sure how I was going to make it through this meeting.

"Right...okay...sorry to keep you waiting." It felt strange hearing him sound nervous after being so confident last night.

"My name's Isaac Sharpe but please call me Isaac." He looked directly at me, "Please remember that I am *not* your teacher. As a personal tutor, I'm just here to help and advise you. Anything that you say to me is strictly confidential."

I got the feeling that he was trying to reassure me about some of the things we had spoken about last night. "I have worked here for two years. I, myself, graduated from this university a few years ago with a degree in business studies."

I felt like he was saying more than he had to for my benefit. It was pretty obvious what he was doing. He was trying to explain himself the best way he could whilst Hollie was in the room.

"Have you got any questions?" he looked at me nervously, waiting for my response. Hollie raised her hand. "You don't have to raise your hand" he told her.

"What kind of things can you help us with?" she asked whilst twirling a strand of her hair.

"A variety of things. Finance, job placements, extracurricular activities..."

Her eyes lit up, "Extracurricular activities sound fun" she purred.

"Yes, the chess club is pretty popular" he replied bluntly.

Oh how I loved his sarcasm.

Hollie took a moment to think about what he had just said before giggling, "That's funny...he's funny isn't he April?"

Isaac's eyes snapped to mine when she mentioned my name.

"Hilarious" I said, looking straight at him. Hollie giggled even more at my response. For a split second, I saw the same sparkle in his eyes that I had seen last night but it quickly faded. It was difficult seeing him this way but I kept telling myself that it was his fault for not telling me that he worked for the university. I wondered whether he had been planning on telling me tonight but now I would never find out.

"I need you both to fill in some paperwork for me." He handed a clipboard over to Hollie and then to me. Our eyes met and I could feel the butterflies in my stomach. I managed to look away but struggled to concentrate filling the forms in. Hollie finished way before me so I had to listen to her flirt shamelessly with him for at least ten minutes. He was blunt with her and mostly gave one word answers but it was still painful to listen to.

My jaw clenched when she complimented him on his fashion sense and proceeded to run her fingers across his chest. He immediately stepped back and looked at me. I placed the forms on his desk, trying my best not to look at either of them.

"Are we done?" I asked whilst looking at the floor.

"Well that depends..." he replied softly.

I closed my eyes and took a deep breath before looking up at him. I knew that he wasn't referring to the meeting.

"On what?" It came out a little harsher than intended.

"Do you want to talk about anything?"

"I don't think there's anything left to say."

He turned and looked at Hollie who was looking confused, "Hollie, if you've not got any further questions, you're free to leave. Thanks for coming."

He was trying to get me alone but it didn't matter what any of us said, the outcome was still going to be the same. He would still be my tutor and I would still be his student. Last night shouldn't have happened.

Hollie stood up and leaned over his desk. What was wrong with this girl?

"It was my pleasure, *sir*. Will you be at the game on Friday night?"

I stood up, ready to leave. She obviously didn't see any issue flirting with staff members but I, on the other hand, wasn't about to embarrass myself any further. I had worked my ass off to get a place on my course so that I could become a social worker. I wasn't about to throw it all away.

"No, I'm not going" he replied.

She pouted at him, "You should come, I'm cheerleading. I always put on a good show."

"I'm busy."

"Another time then." She flashed her fake smile before walking out of the room, ignoring me completely.

When the door closed behind her, I couldn't bring myself to move. Isaac's voice made me jump, "April, please let me explain."

I should have sat back down and addressed the problem like an adult. I should have talked to him about it and listened to what he had to say. I should have stopped being so goddamn stubborn.

I should have done a lot of things different that day. But instead, I walked out of the door and didn't look back.

Chapter Six

I turned the volume up on my iPod and walked to the coffee shop, trying my best to block out what had just happened. Images of last night flashed through my mind and I felt like screaming in frustration. It was just my luck to want someone who was off limits.

When I arrived, I spotted Lukas straight away. I didn't feel like talking but I was pleased that he was there, maybe he could take my mind off Isaac. I sat down next to him and tried to act as normal as I could.

He looked happy to see me, "Did you change your mind?"

I nodded.

"What's wrong?" he asked, putting his coffee down.

"Nothing, I'm just tired."

His eyes narrowed, "Are you sure? You can talk to me."

Rather than keep insisting that I was okay, I decided to tell him part of the truth, "Hollie has the same tutor as me. She was there just now, she's a total bitch."

He placed his hand on top of mine which felt a little strange but also comforting.

"Don't let her bother you, she's insecure and jealous."

I laughed, "Jealous of what exactly?"

"You. Everything about you."

"I doubt it but thanks for trying to cheer me up."

"I'm telling you the truth, she feels threatened by you." He stood up, "I'm buying you a coffee, what do you like to drink?"

I smiled at his kindness, "I like to drink wine...but a cappuccino's good thanks."

Ten minutes later, we made our way to our next lecture. We sat together and made a tally of the number of times the Professor said the word 'ultimately'. It made me giggle and helped to keep my mind off Isaac. After the lecture, Lukas offered to walk me home.

"Are you sure?" he asked, after I had told him that I would be okay for the second time.

"I'm sure, see you tomorrow."

He nodded, "I'll save you a seat."

As soon as I was by myself, my thoughts were once again consumed by Isaac. I felt like crying when I thought about how happy I was this morning compared to how I was feeling now. I considered going back to his office and talking to him but there really wasn't much point. It wasn't as if anything could happen between us now. Plus, I was still angry at him for not telling me last night.

By the time I got home, I was well and truly miserable. I emptied my bag and checked my phone. I had two missed calls, one from Katie and the other from Isaac. He had tried calling me this morning, before I even went to the meeting. Was he calling about our date tonight or to confess? I also had a text message from him, sent an hour ago -

"April, is our meeting tonight still going ahead as planned?"

My jaw hit the ground as I stared at the screen. By meeting, did he mean the date? Did he still think that it was going ahead? Surely not. Maybe he just wanted to talk seeing as though I didn't give him the chance earlier. As much as I wanted to see him, everything was different now.

"It's not necessary."

Within a minute he replied -

"If you change your mind, you know where I am."

Yes, he would be in his office at the university because that's where he *works*.

I switched on the TV and painted my nails to try and take my mind off things but of course, it didn't work. When Katie rang me an hour later, I told her everything.

"Wow...." she said, after I had finally stopped talking.

48

"I know."

"That's awesome."

"Wait, what?"

"What an absolute turn on. You need to text him right now and tell him that you've changed your mind about tonight. Do it. Why aren't you doing it?"

"Katie, stop. This is not awesome, it's the opposite of awesome. He's my tutor and he hid it from me."

"Big deal if he's your tutor. From what you've just told me, you're practically in love with the dude. He didn't hide it from you, it just didn't come up."

"Well it should have come up. He thought that it was important to tell me that he plays the piano but not that he works for the university? I'm sorry but he didn't tell me on purpose, he knew that I was a student."

"Did he though? Did you actually tell him that you were?"

I thought about it for a minute, "Well, no..."

"You thought he was a student, what if he thought you were staff?"

I sighed, "That's not the same thing."

"Hey, I'm just putting it out there. You won't know what he was thinking unless you talk to him. You've got to admit, the whole student-teacher thing is hot."

When I didn't respond, she started laughing. "See, it's h-o-t."

"It's still a crappy situation. I thought you'd understand."

"Don't be like that, I do understand. I just think you're taking it too seriously."

"I should be taking it seriously. People get sacked and kicked off courses for stuff like this. Even if I wanted to date him, I couldn't."

"I'm sure there are ways around it."

"Like me being completely oblivious to it? How long would he have kept it from me?"

"Okay, what if he would have told you last night? Then what?" she asked.

"Well I wouldn't have gone into the park with him for starters."

"Hmmm, I've got to admit, even I think that was stupid."

I ignored her and carried on, "I wouldn't have danced with him or swapped numbers."

"He's still the same person, he just happens to work at your university. He obviously didn't know that he was your tutor last night so maybe you should cut him some slack. He probably didn't want to scare you off by telling you that he worked there. You've even admitted that you would have acted differently around him if you would have known."

I didn't know what to say, maybe she was right. If he didn't tell me because he didn't want to scare me off then would I still be mad at him? It was obvious that he was upset by the situation this afternoon.

"April, you know I'm here for you and I'll always be on your side. But please think about it before you shut him out completely. I want you to be happy and if I'm being honest, I've never heard you talk about a guy like this before. At least talk to him about it."

"I'll think about it."

"At least sleep with him before you get rid."

"Katie! That's not helping!"

"Sorry...actually no, I'm not sorry."

"I'm hanging up. You should go and sit in the naughty corner and think about what you've done."

"I will, as long as you think about talking to him."

"Bye."

"Text me if you talk to him."

50

"Bye" I repeated.

She blew a raspberry down the phone before saying bye and hanging up.

I took Katie's advice and spent most of the night thinking about him, changing my mind back and forth. I thought about the way that I had felt last night when I was dancing with him and how happy I had been this morning. I picked my phone up at one point, intending to call him but then reality hit me and all that I could think about was sitting in his office today. It all seemed screwed up. There was no possible way that anything could happen between us. I finally came to the conclusion that I should just appreciate the situation for what it was. We had one amazing night together but that's all it was ever going to be.

I went to bed reminding myself over and over that I moved here to study, not to be distracted by a man. A man who was incredibly hot, funny and intelligent. A man who gave me butterflies.

Chapter Seven

"I mean this in the nicest way possible but you look tired. Late night?" Lukas asked.

I rubbed my eyes, hoping that it might wake me up a little. "Something like that" I replied as we sat down in our first seminar of the term. I was looking forward to asking questions and actually discussing the topics instead of just taking notes like we did in the lectures.

"Sounds intriguing..."

"It's really not." I didn't tell him that I looked tired because I was completely drained from dreaming about Isaac all night. Every time I woke up, I fell straight back to sleep and dreamt about him again. There was no escaping him. Although my dreams were pleasant, it made it ten times worse to wake up and remember that I couldn't be with him.

Lukas searched my face for a moment before I looked away, paranoid that he would somehow figure out why I was so tired.

"Are you okay? You seemed down yesterday."

"I didn't sleep very well last night, I'll be fine after some coffee."

He nodded, finally taking his searching eyes away from mine.

The Professor made us work in small groups and gave us all discussion topics. I was in a group with Lukas and three other students who were all very chatty and confident. It was saying something when I was actually the quiet one in the group. I started thinking about Katie and how the others wouldn't get a word in edge ways if she was here. She always made herself heard, even if it meant shouting.

I felt his presence immediately. I'd like to put it down to instinct and gut feelings but I think it probably had more to do with the fact that the majority of females in the class were whispering and giggling. I looked up to see Isaac talking to the Professor.

There really was no escaping him.

Why did he have to be so goddamn handsome? It would be

much easier to forget about him if he didn't look quite so edible. I could see Lukas watching him out of the corner of my eye.

"Isn't that the guy who you were talking to at the mixer?" he asked.

"Yep" I said, not wanting to discuss it any further. I had already spent too much time thinking about him last night...and this morning...and three seconds ago.

Lucy turned to face me, "Do you know him?"

I nodded, "He's my tutor."

I noticed Lukas's face soften.

She smirked, "You lucky thing. He can *tutor* me anytime."

My heart leapt and then sank when the Professor called my name, "April, Mr Sharpe would like to talk to you."

I could feel the heat rising in my cheeks as I just sat there and stared at Isaac. My legs didn't seem to be working properly. What did he want to talk to me about? Could he not have waited until after the seminar?

Lukas nudged me and I watched Isaac noticeably stiffen at our contact.

"I think he's waiting for you. What's it about?"

I shrugged, "I guess I'm about to find out."

I finally managed to stand up and walk to the front of the classroom. One girl winked at me on my way out. I rolled my eyes in response. Isaac held the door open for me and then closed it behind us.

"I'm sorry to interrupt your seminar. How are you?" he asked.

I turned to face him, "I've been better. What's this about?"

"Straight to business, huh?"

"I'm straight to the point, unlike *some* people."

53

"So you're still mad at me then?"

"I'm not mad."

"Is this where you say that you're not mad but you've actually got a dartboard with my face on it?"

I wanted to smile. Hell, I wanted to do a lot of things but you don't always get what you want.

"I'm not mad" I repeated.

"Well that's a good start. Now will you please let me explain about the other night?"

I sighed, "Is that why you've taken me out of my seminar? Because this isn't the time or the place."

"So tell me when and where."

I took a deep breath, "Look, you don't need to explain anything. This doesn't have to be any more embarrassing than it already is."

"Embarrassing? I'm not embarrassed. I'm scared. Scared that you don't want anything to do with me anymore."

"*I'm* scared that I don't want anything to do with you anymore" I whispered.

"Great, so we're both scared. Let me make you feel better."

"Isaac..."

"I love hearing you say my name."

Just like I loved it when he said mine. He caressed each syllable making it sound almost erotic.

"I can't do this now..."

"Come to a lecture with me on Friday night."

"Is that what they're calling it these days?"

A small smile crept across his face, "Now there's the April that

I remember."

I looked down at the floor and shuffled my feet, "What lecture is it?"

"It's all about social work, a friend of mine is a guest speaker. I thought you might be interested."

I thought for a long moment before answering. It did sound like it would be helpful and I would be lying if I said that I didn't want to spend more time with him. But my feelings for him were so strong that I didn't know if I could trust myself to be alone with him. If something was to happen, would I be able to say no? I needed to be sensible.

"Thanks for the invite but I can't, I'm busy."

"Doing what?"

His question threw me. I desperately tried to come up with an excuse and said the first thing that popped into my head, "I'm actually going to the game."

He started to laugh.

"What's so funny?" I asked.

"I would never have guessed that you like football."

"Well I would never have guessed that you were my tutor."

"April..."

"I've got to get back to class."

I walked away from him, mad at myself for not going to the stupid lecture with him and then mad at myself for even thinking that way. My heart was telling me to turn back around but my head was screaming at me to carry on walking.

"You can't run away forever" I heard him say quietly.

Maybe not. But I could sure as hell try.

***

My head was spinning when I sat back down in class. Some of

the girls were still looking at me with goofy grins, obviously unaware that he was my tutor. Unless they knew and shared the same opinion as Katie.

"What was that about?" Lukas asked. I could see Lucy and a few others trying to eavesdrop.

"Nothing, we just needed to clarify a couple of things."

"Well I hope it's sorted now."

I nodded, "It is."

Liar.

"What are you doing on Friday night?"

He shrugged, "I've not got anything planned."

"Good because we're going to the game."

"Cool" he replied. That's what I liked about Lukas, he was so laid back.

Lucy wiggled her eyebrows up and down at me.

"Wanna come?" I asked her.

She smiled wider, "How could I say no? Football players are hot."

Chapter Eight

Friday night arrived without hearing another word from Isaac. I wondered whether he had finally realised that nothing was ever going to happen between us. I still dreamt about him every night which was kind of exciting but even more frustrating at the same time.

Although I had never been the biggest football fan, I was still looking forward to the game. It was the first game of the new season so it was a big deal and by the sounds of it, the whole university was going to watch.

I walked to the game with Lukas and we met everyone else there. Lucy came with a couple of her friends and I recognised Dan and a few other guys.

It was only a small stadium with metal bleachers but the noise was deafening. There was music playing for the cheerleaders to dance to as well as a full brass band and people playing the drums in the stands. Nearly everybody wore a Manchester University t-shirt or hoodie and were in high spirits.

After she had finished cheering, Hollie made her way over to us. She said hello to all of the boys and then focused her attention on Lukas, "I'm glad you could make it, did you like my cheer routines?"

"I wasn't watching" he replied.

"More of a reason to come and watch me next week then or I can always give you a private showing later."

"No thanks."

"What's wrong? Are cheerleaders not your thing? I can take the outfit off you know..."

"*You're* not my thing."

I was pretty shocked at how blunt he was being and quite honestly wondered why he seemed to get so bothered by her. She might be a bitch to me but she was nice to him.

"Don't knock it till you've tried it" she said before turning her attention to Dan, much to his delight. "What are you doing later, handsome?" Within a minute or so, they were walking off in the direction of the car park. Dan looked over his shoulder and put his thumbs up.

"Are you okay?" I asked Lukas.

He bumped my shoulder with his, "Yeah, I'm good. I just don't like what kind of person she is."

"Well Dan's done us all a favour."

"I'm sure he will be giving her more than a favour" he added. I shook my head at the thought.

The football players finally got into their positions and the referee blew the whistle to signal the start of the game. I was shocked at how fast paced it was and it wasn't long before both teams had scored a goal each.

The first half went by really quickly and I was surprised at how much I was enjoying it. We watched as the players left the pitch.

Lucy leaned over and tapped me on the shoulder, "Which one have you got your eye on?"

I laughed, "I can't really see their faces."

"Who said anything about their faces? It's all about the body, look at his thighs!"

"Number 7 is cute" chirped one of her friends.

"Okay, it's time for me to get some beers" Lukas said, whilst shaking his head.

We all laughed, "Sorry, do you need some help?" I asked him.

"No it's okay, look who's back" he nodded at Dan who was making his way back over to us.

"That was quick" Lucy muttered.

I had suspected that Dan was a man-whore but what he shouted next confirmed it, "Dude, she's an 8 out of 10, you should totally get some!"

I should have been shocked by his comment but I actually

wasn't. I was more embarrassed when everybody who was in earshot turned around to look at us.

"Dan, shut up for once in your life and help me get the beers."

"I can definitely use a beer, I worked up quite a sweat" he replied.

I watched them walk away before turning my attention back to Lucy. She was shaking her head in disgust and I wondered if it was aimed at Dan or Hollie or both. Her friends were still ogling the last few players left on the pitch. They had moved on from thighs and were now admiring number elevens biceps. One of them wolf whistled, "Forget the football players, I'll have some of *him*." She pointed at somebody standing at the bottom of the bleachers.

He looked insanely attractive and insanely out of place in a shirt and tie.

Isaac.

As much as I tried to keep calm, my heart was beating stupidly fast like it always did whenever he was around. I bent down to pretend to tie my shoelace, hoping that he wouldn't see me.

"That's April's tutor" said Lucy.

"No way! Can you get me his number?" asked her blonde friend. I should really make more of an effort to remember people's names.

I sat back up, "What is wrong with you people? He's my *tutor*."

"He's gorgeous."

Tell me something I don't know.

I took a deep breath and looked down at where he had been standing. To my surprise, he was gone. I felt relieved and disappointed at the same time. That's when I felt my phone vibrate. I fished it out of my pocket and stared at the new text message from Isaac -

"Meet me at the gates in 5 minutes or I'm coming back in."

I sighed and stood up, blocking out what the girls were saying about him. Or rather, what they wanted to do to him. It was becoming blatantly obvious that I didn't like it when other girls talked about him.

"I'll be back in a minute." I made my way down the bleachers and over towards the main entrance gates. When I got there, I could see him waiting for me. He was leaning against the wall, deep in thought. He looked so sexy with his sleeves rolled up and his tie loosened.

"Did you miss the memo about the dress code?" I asked as we came face to face.

He smiled, "I always like to look my best. Will you walk with me?"

I looked at my watch and it suddenly reminded me of the first time we met. "The second half starts in ten minutes" I said shakily.

"This won't take long."

We walked side by side down the long road leading away from the stadium.

"You like stealing me away don't you?"

"I don't know what you mean" he replied.

"First you stole me away from the mixer, then the seminar and now the game."

"I told you that I don't like to share."

I blushed, "I thought you were going to your friends lecture tonight?"

"I left early."

"Why?"

"April, you're an intelligent girl. Work it out."

I wanted to run. I wanted to turn around and literally run away from him. I was a fast runner, he even said so himself.

"Don't even think about it..."

"Think about what?" I asked.

"Bailing on me. I'll sling you over my shoulder if I have to." I knew that he was telling the truth. "How are you?" he asked.

"I'm fine."

He raised his eyebrow and looked down at me with his impossibly blue eyes, "You might try and lie to yourself but please don't lie to me."

My heart sped up. "What exactly do you want me to say Isaac? That the other night was one of the best nights of my life? That I can't stop thinking about you? That I dream about you? What good is all of that? You're my tutor. This is real life, I can't do this."

"Can't or won't?"

I thought for a long time before answering. I knew that what I was about to say would change everything. I took a deep breath.

"Won't."

The pain in his eyes destroyed me. He spoke slowly and I could hear the raw emotion in his voice, "If that's what you really want then I'll walk away now. But you need to know that it's not what I want. I would fight for you, for *us*."

I could feel the tears beginning to sting my eyes. I felt like screaming and telling him that it wasn't what I really wanted. I wanted him. I wanted him desperately. But I was in way over my head. I was overwhelmed and scared and I hated feeling so vulnerable. I was alone in a new city at a new university and my whole future depended on this. I did the total opposite of what he asked me to do, I lied to him.

"It's what I want."

He shook his head, "I don't believe you and I don't think that you believe it either. But right now, I've got to listen to what you're telling me."

I watched him walk away and couldn't hold back the tears any longer. I wanted to tell him to stop, to come back. I opened my mouth but no sound came out. I let myself cry before taking a deep breath, wiping my face and pretending that it never happened. After all, how could something hurt me if it never happened in the first place? This was the best thing to do.

He was right, I did lie to myself.

***

I got back to the game just after the second half had started. I had to battle through the crowd to get back to Lukas and the others. Everybody was engrossed in the game except for Lukas, who was focusing all of his attention on me.

"Hey, are you okay?" he asked.

I nodded.

"Are you sure?"

"I wasn't feeling too good but I'll be okay."

"Do you want me to take you home? I don't mind."

"No, let's stay and watch the rest of the game."

Lucy turned around from her seat in front, "Where's your hot tutor gone?"

I shrugged, pretending to focus on the game.

"Oh, is your tutor here?" Lukas asked.

"We saw him walk by at half time" I replied.

"You seemed to get along well at the mixer, did you know him before you started here?"

No. Five days ago, Isaac didn't even exist in my world and now he consumed it. How was it possible that one person could change everything?

"No, we were just talking about the course."

I bit my lip and tried my best to think about something else. Number elevens biceps didn't seem to be working. Lukas nodded and thankfully didn't ask any more questions.

62

I did a pretty good job pretending that nothing was wrong for the rest of the game. I joined in with the clapping and cheering and celebrated when our team won. Everybody was going for celebratory drinks afterwards but I wanted to go home. I needed to be alone. I had nothing to celebrate.

I didn't know how much longer I could pretend to be okay.

Chapter Nine

The next two weeks consisted of eating lots of ice cream, perfecting my fake smile and checking my phone every single hour without fail. I didn't see or hear a word from Isaac apart from every night in my dreams. I would dream about us being happy together and then wake up feeling emotionally drained. I used to look forward to going to sleep so that I could see him but now I dreaded going to sleep. I knew that it was my choice not to be with him but I couldn't decide if that made it easier or harder.

Most days, it was difficult to concentrate in class and when I wasn't in class, I was worried in case I bumped into him on campus. I had to give it to Lukas though, he did a good job of distracting me. We grew close and I enjoyed spending time with him. He made me feel at ease when I was with him which made me want to be around him even more. The amount of time that we were spending together caused some whispering but I didn't care. He made me feel better and no problem seemed half as bad when I was around him. He was like my very own security blanket.

I think he had sensed that something was going on with me and invited me out nearly every night. I had gone for drinks with him and some other people off our course a few times but passed on most invitations. However, I had agreed to go out for something to eat tonight as I couldn't face being home alone on a Friday night.

My heart leapt when my phone rang, like it did every other time since I last saw Isaac. I should have known it wouldn't be him but deep down, I still expected him to call.

"Hey Kitty" I said as I picked up.

"What are you crazy kids up to tonight? Going to some swanky club?"

"Nah, I'm just going for something to eat with Lukas."

"Hmmm, just you two?"

"Yes."

"So it's a date?"

"No."

"Oh my god, it's totally a date! Why didn't you tell me?"

"Because it's not a date, we're just going for some food. Calm down."

"Oh come on, you're always in a group but tonight it's just you two which means it's a date. Do you like him?"

With everything that was going on with Isaac, I hadn't even thought about him in that way. He was good looking but we were just good friends.

"We're just friends" I told her.

"Does he know that?"

"Yeah. Well, I think so."

"He seems nice."

"He is nice."

"But?"

"But...he's not...he's not my type."

"You mean he's not Isaac?"

"Don't bring him into it. Please can we talk about something else."

"We can but I don't want to..."

"Then you can hang up and let me finish getting ready."

"Don't be like that, I'm sorry. How are you doing anyway?"

"I'm fine."

"And I'm your best friend. How are you really doing?"

"I have my good days and my bad days."

"Are you still having the dreams?"

"Every night."

"You know that it doesn't have to be this way, you have a choice."

"Do I?"

"Of course you do."

"Well even if I did change my mind, it's too late now. Isaac's moved on."

"How do you know?"

"Well I've not heard from him."

"April, you told the poor guy that you didn't want anything to happen between you two. He's giving you the space that you asked for."

"Yeah, well...I really need to get ready. I'll call you tomorrow."

"Okay. I hope you have fun tonight, make sure you're both on the same page."

I thought about what she had said right up until Lukas picked me up. I had never thought about him in that way but in all honesty, that was probably because of Isaac. If I had never met Isaac, would I have been attracted to Lukas in that way? He was a genuinely nice guy after all and seemed to care about me. I tried to put it to the back of my mind and just have fun.

***

The Italian quickly became one of my favourite restaurants in town. It was inviting and authentic and the food was to die for. But there was one problem. After my conversation with Katie, I felt different around Lukas. It was strange but I found myself looking at him a little longer than I usually did. Lukas was just his same usual self which convinced me that of course it wasn't a date, we were just hanging out without the others.

"Thanks for tonight, this place is awesome."

"Any time" he replied. "There's an equally awesome Chinese restaurant just down the road, maybe we could go there next time?"

Next time?

"Are you going to ask the others to come too?"

He cocked his head to one side, "Yeah, I asked them tonight but they were all busy."

See, it wasn't a date. I nodded and there was an awkward silence between us.

"So...do you want me to?" he asked.

"Want you to what?"

"Ask the others next time?"

"Yes...no...I don't mind." Then something strange happened - I blushed. I had never felt embarrassed around him before and now I felt self-conscious all of a sudden. Damn Katie putting stupid ideas into my head, that girl was dangerous.

He laughed, "Your answer was very helpful." He thought for a moment, "I see Dan every single day so maybe I won't invite him."

We see each other every single day too...

I shrugged, "Whatever."

"It's nice having some time away from Dan...and spending time with you obviously."

I nodded, "It's different when we're in a big group."

He looked thoughtful, "Can I ask you a question?"

"Sure."

"Is there anything that you want to talk about?"

My heart started beating faster.

"No, why?"

"I've noticed that some days you can be in a really good mood and others you seem upset like something's bothering you."

"Oh...um..."

"You don't have to say anything, I just want you to know that I'm here for you. You can talk to me."

I looked directly into his warm chocolatey eyes, "Thank you, I appreciate it."

After an awkward silence, he spoke, "I would appreciate some ice cream right about now."

***

"I can't believe that you ate it all."

He held his hands up, "What can I say? I like ice cream."

We were on our way back to my house. The night was cool but the rain had stopped. The sky was clear and I loved being able to look up and see all of the stars twinkling down at me.

"What are you doing tomorrow?" he asked.

"Coursework, boringggg."

"Do you want to come to a party?"

"Whose party?"

"Just some guy that I know, he's cool. It's nothing big. You should come."

"I'm not sure, maybe."

"I know what maybe means. What can I do to make you say yes?"

I looked up and caught his eye. He looked playful but I couldn't tell if he was being flirty. I was probably being paranoid. I looked away quickly, not having a clue how to answer his question.

"I'll come."

"Well that was easy, you could have taken advantage then."

Every now and then, the Scottish in his accent would come out

68

and I couldn't help but think how sexy it sounded. I looked down, feeling a little flushed. Why was I feeling this way? Was I trying to force myself to feel something more for Lukas to make up for losing Isaac?

"Text me the address and I'll be there" I told him as we stopped outside my house.

"Well I'll swing by about seven if that's okay and we can go down together."

"Okay, well...I guess I'll see you tomorrow."

Ordinarily, I might have invited him in for a coffee but my brain wasn't working properly tonight. I was feeling too many emotions which was making me act like a total idiot.

"Goodnight," he said as he pulled me into a hug. I had been craving some comfort so it felt nice being in his arms. I'm pretty sure that it lasted longer than the average friendly hug was supposed to last. I pulled away and looked up at him. I didn't know if it was the alcohol or my emotions playing with me but I felt like I was looking at him in a whole new light. Standing in front of me was a kind, funny, intelligent man. He was a genuinely good person and I could actually picture myself settling down with somebody like him in the future. I needed to get out of there before I got even more confused about everything.

"Goodnight" I said.

When I got inside, I slumped down on the sofa and let my mind wander. Within minutes, I let sleep wash over me.

Once again, I woke up feeling even more tired than before. I was still on the sofa and my cheeks were streaked with mascara. Some nights I dreamt about losing Isaac, but the most upsetting dreams were when we were impossibly happy together. The fact that I was still dreaming about him could only mean one thing. I was fighting.

I wasn't ready to let him go.

Chapter Ten

I spent the whole of Saturday reading and doing coursework so by the time seven rolled around, I was actually looking forward to the party. I warned myself not to act like a complete idiot around Lukas again.

When there was a knock on my door, I opened it to see him leaning against the door frame with a grin on his face. My eyes quickly roamed his body, he looked good. He had done something different to his hair, spiked it up.

"Your hair."

He waited for me to say something else but when I didn't he laughed, "Yes, this is my hair."

"I meant that it looks different...nice."

What did I say about not acting like an idiot?

He grinned, "I thought it was time for a change. You look wonderful, as always."

I blushed, "Thanks." I hadn't even put much thought into my outfit, deciding on a pair of jeans and a simple black vest top to match my black stiletto heels.

"You ready to go?" he asked.

"Yep." I locked the door behind me and put my keys into my handbag, along with my phone and lip gloss - the essentials. I was expecting to walk so when I saw the taxi pulled up outside, I looked up at him questioningly.

"Your carriage awaits." He smiled and held the door open for me.

I climbed inside and waited for him to get in. "I thought we were going to walk?"

"Yeah well it's cold out tonight and I guessed that you would be wearing heels."

I looked into his warm eyes, impressed by how thoughtful and considerate he had been. I couldn't think of any other guy who would think like that. Well, except maybe one.

"Well thank you, you know how to treat a lady right."

He looked around, "There's a lady here?"

I scowled at him, "I take that back."

His laughter was interrupted by the taxi driver, "Where to guys? The meters running."

***

We walked into the party and was greeted by several people from our course. I couldn't help but notice that Hollie was also there, talking to Dan. That's if nibbling on each other's ears counted as talking. They actually seemed like a good match.

"Please keep me away from her" I whispered to Lukas, nodding in her direction.

"My pleasure."

We went and got ourselves a drink from the kitchen. They had pretty much every drink that you could think of, it looked like somebody had robbed a liquor store. I decided on Jack Daniels and coke. Lukas introduced me to some other people that he knew and we ended up chatting in the kitchen for at least an hour. This turned out to be a good idea as we were far away from Hollie but bad as we were in reaching distance of the alcohol.

Two hours and several shots later, I was having an awesome time. Me and Lukas had managed to make complete fools of ourselves by dancing with blow up dolls but I couldn't stop smiling. The night was going really well. Too well. I blame what happened next on the shots.

Hollie and Dan made their way over to us.

"I'm ready to leave if you are" I muttered to Lukas under my breath.

"Hi, good looking" Hollie said.

I rolled my eyes but felt light headed so grabbed on to Lukas

71

to steady myself. He looked at my hand on his arm and then up to meet my eyes.

"Are you okay?"

I smiled sheepishly, "Yeah, looks like I've had too many shots."

"Do you want me to take you home?"

"Oh no you don't." Hollie grabbed Lukas by the other arm and pulled him to her. "The only place that you're going is home with me."

I shouldn't have been, but I was shocked by her behaviour. I thought that she must have been really drunk to act this way but then she acted like this when she was sober too. I thought back to the football game where she had disappeared into the car park with Dan. He had been quite vocal about what had happened. What kind of girl does that?

Lukas looked disgusted at her and pulled away, "Have some self respect."

She laughed at him, "Have some fun, you're so uptight."

I glanced at Dan, wondering what he must be thinking about her behaviour but he just looked amused. Maybe he was one of those 'caring is sharing' kind of guys?

What she did next really pissed me off. Not just because I cared about Lukas but because she was giving women in general a bad name. She leant forwards and quite blatantly rubbed Lukas's crotch. I saw red. "Get your fucking hand off him *now*."

All three of them turned towards me looking shocked. I moved closer to her so that I was right in her face. She dropped her hand but kept her eyes locked with mine. I was so angry, who does she think she is?

"Stop being such a degrading little whore. No means no. Just because he's a guy doesn't automatically mean that he wants you to touch him. Do us all a favour and go home."

She smiled and slowly began to clap. I realised that the room had fallen silent and everybody was watching us.

"Is this the part where I'm supposed to cry? Nice try but I've heard it all before."

"No, this is the part where you're supposed to open your eyes and see what everybody else sees. You're such a stuck up little bitch, going around thinking that you're better than everybody else." I looked around the room, "Everybody thinks it, they just won't admit it. They probably feel sorry for you. You're so cheap and desperate."

Lukas placed his hand on my shoulder, "Come on, I think it's time to leave."

"Wait" she said, before throwing her glass of wine in my face, "now it's time to leave."

I could hear everybody around us talking and whispering as I picked up a napkin and wiped my face. I was so angry, I felt like I was going to explode.

"Your mother must be so proud of you" I told her before turning around and walking out, not even stopping when I got outside.

"April, wait" Lukas shouted. I slowed down until he was walking beside me. He grabbed my hand and gently squeezed it. It felt warm and comforting. My head was spinning from all of the alcohol and I was still infuriated with Hollie. Add this to lack of sleep and the whole Isaac situation and I was one big ball of raw emotion. I burst into tears and sat down on the pavement.

"Hey, don't cry" he said as he wrapped his arms around me.

"I'm so angry with her."

"I know, me too. What you said back there, every single word of it was true. She needed to hear it. But you can't let her upset you."

"I'm not upset, I'm just angry and confused."

"Confused about what?"

"Everything. I'm tired of feeling this way."

Our eyes met and before I even had time to think about it, I kissed him. After he got over the shock, he reciprocated the kiss. Our mouths worked together and in that moment, I forgot about everything else. His tongue darted in and out of my mouth and before long, the kiss turned fiery. My hands explored his chest whilst I sucked on his tongue. I stopped when I remembered where we were. When I pulled away, we were both left gasping for air. Had that just happened? More importantly, what else might have happened if we weren't in public?

We were quiet for a long time before I looked at him and we both started to laugh.

"Well I wasn't expecting that" he said with a huge grin on his face.

"Me neither."

"Where did it come from?"

I shrugged, "I'm sorry for attacking you like that."

"Don't be. I quite enjoy being attacked by you."

I smiled and stood up, swaying until Lukas grabbed hold of me. "I think I need to sleep this alcohol off."

"Good idea" he replied.

"It's a good job I didn't wear white."

"Huh?"

I looked down at my wet top, "The wine..."

He groaned, "I'm sorry about that."

"Why are you sorry? You didn't do it."

"No but you didn't deserve it."

"It just shows how much of a bitch she is. I mean, what sort of person throws a drink in somebody's face?"

"You were pretty amazing back there you know."

I blushed, unsure what he was actually referring to.

"You stood up to her, it's about time she heard the truth."

"Yeah well she was way out of order touching you like that."

He nodded, "I was going to say something but you beat me to it."

"I couldn't stop myself. She definitely crossed the line tonight. What's up with Dan? He just stood there looking like he found it funny that she was groping you after he had made out with her all night."

"Who knows what Dan thinks in that tiny little pea brain of his."

"I get that she's an easy lay but he shouldn't try so hard to pimp her out to you, it's gross."

"Let's just forget about both of them."

"I'm not sure if I can. I'm never going to be able to look at wine the same way again."

"I could say the same about you."

I looked up at him questioningly.

"The kiss."

I blushed, "I know we're friends. I'm sorry if I've...complicated things."

"April, you've got nothing to be sorry about."

"I think I'm going to throw up..."

He chuckled, "I'm glad I have that effect on you."

"It's not you, I'm never doing shots again."

"Yeah yeah, I've heard it all before."

I groaned, "The sad thing is, I've said it all before. I never learn my lesson."

"Come on, let's get you home to bed."

"Wait, I've been meaning to ask you something..." He looked at me with a serious expression. "Can I have a piggy back? My feet are killing me."

He smiled, "Jump on."

I didn't know why I had kissed him but I was glad that we were still able to act normal around each other. The last thing I wanted to do was lose Lukas as a friend.

When we finally got back to mine, he was a real gentleman. He poured me a glass of water and tucked me into bed, leaving a bucket next to me in case I needed to be sick.

After asking me at least half a dozen times if I was going to be alright, he locked the door and posted the key back through the letter box.

To my surprise, I wasn't sick once. In fact, I slept like a baby.

Chapter Eleven

For the first time in a long time, I didn't dream about Isaac. Or at least, I couldn't remember dreaming about him. It felt like some kind of breakthrough for me. I was about to text Katie the good news when memories of last night came flooding back to me. I groaned when I remembered my argument with Hollie. Even though she deserved my rant, I regretted saying some things. Not because I felt bad about actually saying them but because I'd rather not have wine thrown in my face in front of a room full of people.

I checked my phone and had a text message from Lukas -

"Is it weird that I like it when you get angry? Hope you're feeling okay today x"

I laughed at his message and then thought about our kiss. There was no denying that we had both enjoyed it but what happens now? Were we supposed to act like it never happened? Did it only happen because we were drunk? I wasn't sure what I wanted with Lukas but I definitely didn't want to lose the friendship that we had. Plus, there was Isaac. One kiss with Lukas wasn't going to make me magically forget all about him. It would take a whole lot more than that. I still had strong feelings for him and I wasn't sure if that was ever going to change. But I had made my decision not to pursue things with him for a reason and I needed to remember that.

After having a shower, I cooked a full English breakfast to try and cure my hangover.

I ate half of it before throwing it back up.

So instead, I called Katie. Just before it went to voicemail, she picked up, "How was your date with Lukas?"

"Hello to you too."

"Hello, how was your date with Lukas?"

"Why don't you get straight to the point next time?"

She laughed, "Well, the suspense has been killing me. I was going to ring you yesterday to get the low down but I got into a big fight with Ian so I ended up going to my mum's."

"Oh no, what happened?"

"Nothing's happening, that's the problem. Since we had Jamie, we hardly ever have sex. All I want is to be a MILF, is that too much to ask for?"

I laughed. A lot.

"I'm glad that you find it funny."

"I'm sorry, it just sounds weird when you say the word MILF in a serious voice. Honestly, you're gorgeous. You're definitely a MILF so stop worrying. I've heard that it's common for couples to cut down on sex after the baby is born. Do you even have time for it?"

"Well not really. That's why when we do get time, I want it. Jeez, it's like I'm the guy in the relationship."

"Well we've always known that. I'm sure things will work out. Go and buy some new underwear and a whip or something, show him who's boss."

"That's a good idea actually...I better not take the baby with me though. Anyway, what happened with you and Lukas?"

I laughed, "Nothing on Friday."

I moved the phone away from my ear when she squealed, "So when?"

"Last night but I'm not sure how I feel about it yet."

"I need details!"

"Well, Friday was kind of awkward thanks to you."

"Oh don't go blaming me. If I wouldn't have mentioned it being a date, you'd still be pining over Isaac now."

The silence gave me away.

She groaned, "You're still pining over him?"

"Maybe a little. But I didn't dream about him last night, that's a good sign right?"

She sighed, "April, you've been dreaming about him for the past two weeks, if anything's a sign then it's definitely that. So what happened with Lukas?"

"We went to a party last night and I was fine until I started doing shots..."

"What did I tell you about shots?"

"That they're the work of the devil."

"And?"

"And never to do them."

"But you decided to do them anyway? I thought that you were the intelligent one."

"Wait, I thought that I'm the cool one? Anyway, everything was going great until I had an argument with Hollie because she groped Lukas"

"I hope you told that bitch a thing or two."

"I did, maybe even three."

"That's my girl."

"But then she threw wine in my face."

"Right, I'm going to drop Jamie off at my mums and come straight over there."

"Thanks but no thanks, I don't want to make things worse."

"*You* won't be doing anything."

"Please just leave it, I think she got the message loud and clear. I called her a degrading whore and told her that her mother must be very proud of her."

"Nice."

"I know. So we left and I was really wound up and basically attacked his mouth."

"So you made the first move?"

"Yep."

"Interesting. How was it?"

"Nice."

"Nice? Can you think of a better adjective to use next time?"

I sighed, "I don't know if there will be a next time."

"Well what happened after you kissed?"

"He walked me home."

"Then what?"

"He put me into bed."

"Then what?"

"I went to sleep and he went home."

"You're so boring!"

"And you're so charming. You've just told me that it's a sign that I've been dreaming about Isaac and now you're disappointed that I didn't sleep with Lukas? You sound even more confused than I am."

"Have you spoken to Lukas today?"

"He text me this morning."

"So he's into you then."

"It was one kiss, nothing's changed."

"Nothing stays the same, baby girl. He's bound to want more. The question is, do you?"

"I don't know what I want."

"I do, but you're way too stubborn to let yourself have it. Do you really want to start something with Lukas when you're mind fucking Isaac every night?"

"I don't even know how to respond to that, I'm going to pretend you didn't say it."

"You need to have a good think about what you want. Remember that you can't sit around waiting for happiness to find you. *You* find *it*."

I laughed.

"What's funny?" she asked.

"You. You give me a hard time but then you come out with something meaningful like that. I don't know what I'd do without you."

"Well you'll never have to find out. Love you."

"Love you too. Talk to you soon, okay?"

"Okay, have fun thinking about Lukas...or Isaac...or both of them at the same time." Her giggle was infectious.

When I got off the phone, I replied to Lukas's text message from earlier -

"Thanks for looking after me last night. Did I mention that I'm never doing shots again? I'm paying for it today! x"

I had a raging headache but was out of paracetamol so decided to walk to the shop to get some. The fresh air would probably do me some good too. I scraped my hair back and put on my coat and converse before heading out. On my way over there, I received another text message from Lukas -

"Yes, you said that shots have something to do with the devil?? I had a lot of fun last night. What are you doing later? Let me know if you need me to come and look after you x"

Oh. I wasn't expecting him to say that. I wasn't in the mood to see anybody today as I wasn't feeling or looking too great but he did have a way of making me feel better. I put my phone back in my pocket, unsure of what to do.

When I got to the shop, I chose some extra strength paracetamol and picked up a few other things before making my way to the till. Before I even got there, the room started to spin and I felt like I was going to be sick. I grabbed on to the nearest shelf and took a few deep breaths. Stupid hangover. I carried on walking and realised why I had suddenly felt so unravelled. I was looking straight at Isaac.

I held my breath. I really didn't want him to see me like this. We stood staring at each other in silence. As if on cue, my heart started pounding and I felt light headed. Please god, don't let me fall over in front of him again. I was hoping that I wouldn't react like this around him anymore after not seeing him for several weeks but that was stupid of me. Was he always going to have this effect on me? I watched as the corners of his mouth turned up into a sad smile. Whoever said that a picture paints a thousand words were talking about moments like this. Everything that had happened between us was reflected in that smile. He looked regretful and I couldn't help but wonder if he regretted ever meeting me.

"Are you going to pay for those?" The cashier asked Isaac. He turned around to face them and I finally let out the breath that I had been holding. Isaac said something back to the cashier which made them laugh. Why did he always have to be so charming?

My stomach was performing somersaults worthy of an Olympic gold medal. It was the strangest thirty seconds of my life. I stood there staring at his back whilst my emotions were exploding like fireworks inside my head. First came sadness, then desire, followed by regret and confusion. I didn't know whether to stay or leave, say something to him or stay quiet. He ended up making those decisions for me.

After paying, he walked out of the shop and didn't look back. I was almost certain that he was going to be waiting for me outside but he wasn't. I tried to get my head around what had just happened. I thought he would have wanted to stay and talk to me, at least say hello. But he just shared a joke with the cashier as if everything was good in the world before leaving. He must be over me. I wished that I could say the same about him. But if he was over me, why did he look so sad? There was no mistaking the sadness in his eyes.

On my way home, I dialled his number five times before cancelling straight away each time. I wanted to talk to him, to hear his voice, to hear that he still wanted me. God, I was messed up.

I made call number six.

Lukas picked up on the second ring, "Hey, how are you feeling?"

"Like crap."

"I'm not surprised."

"Why?"

"All the alcohol you drank last night."

"Oh, yeah."

Of course he was talking about the alcohol. Lukas didn't know that the main reason I felt like crap was because of Isaac.

"Where are you?" he asked.

"I'm walking home from the shop. Do you want to come over to mine later?"

He paused, long enough to make me doubt what I was doing. "What time?" he asked.

"Give me about an hour."

"Okay, see you then."

I wasn't sure why I had invited Lukas over. But what I did know was that he was awesome at cheering me up and that's exactly what I needed right now. I also needed to let Isaac go once and for all. I had been keeping the memory of him alive in my head and in my dreams but I couldn't do it anymore. It was exhausting. If I was ever going to have a shot at being in a healthy relationship then I needed to let him go.

When I got home, I got changed into something more presentable before sitting down and waiting for Lukas to arrive. The paracetamol had kicked in so at least it didn't feel like somebody was stamping on my head anymore. I didn't have a clue how tonight was going to pan out but I wanted things to be normal between us like they were before the kiss. If something more was to happen between us then fair enough, but I didn't want to force it.

I stared at my phone, half expecting Isaac to call but he didn't.

I knew that I had no right to be angry at him but it seemed a little harsh not even saying hello to me. Talk about extremes, one minute he was pulling me out of seminars and away from football games and the next minute he wouldn't even talk to me. My head was telling me that it was the right thing for both of us but my heart was saying the opposite. My heart craved him.

I tried my best to push all thoughts of Isaac aside when there was a knock on my door. I couldn't keep a straight face when I saw Lukas standing in the hallway wearing a bright orange onesie.

"What?" he asked with a goofy smile.

I shook my head, "You're crazy. Come in quick before my neighbours see you."

"Don't you like it?" he asked when I closed the door behind him.

"I like it. It's very...bright. But I must say, I don't know anybody who wears one in public. Is it a Scottish thing?"

"No, wearing a kilt is a Scottish thing. I'll wear one next time, I think you'll like it better than the onesie."

"Will I now?" I laughed and he nodded, a glint of playfulness in his eyes.

"So how many people saw you wearing this?"

"One, the taxi driver."

I grinned, "You got a taxi, good choice."

"It's really comfortable, you should buy one."

"What? A taxi?" I asked.

"You're so funny."

"I don't even try. Imagine if I did..."

"Please don't, I can't take much more." He laughed and lifted up the bag that he was holding.

I eyed it suspiciously, "What's in the bag?"

"Well seeing as though we're both hung over, I've brought some essentials."

He began to lift the items out of the bag one by one.

I nodded, "Soup...good choice."

"I've put a lot of thought into this. Of course, you can't have soup without..." he pointed at me to answer.

"A bowl?"

He grinned then shook his head, "Not the answer I was looking for." He lifted a stick of French Bread out of the bag.

"We also have Lucozade, you know, for energy."

I raised an eyebrow at him before sitting down on the sofa, "What else have you got in your bag of tricks?"

"The rest is naughty..." his accent curled around the last word, making it sound naughty in itself.

"How so?"

"You know...whips, chains, handcuffs. Like I said, the essentials."

I laughed, thinking how funny it would be if he was actually telling the truth. He lifted out some popcorn and chocolate followed by a selection of movies.

"Very naughty, I'm on a diet."

"Well that's just ridiculous, you're gorgeous."

I blushed and looked down at my feet, "I'm up for watching a movie if you are."

"Sounds good, you can choose."

I ended up choosing a Liam Neeson movie as I was in the mood to watch him kick some ass. We shared the popcorn and high fived during the parts where he was a total bad ass. When it finished, he turned to me, looking like he had something on his mind.

"Should we talk about what happened last night?"

I shrugged, "If you want to. We both had a lot to drink. I really enjoyed myself but I don't want anything to ruin what we've got."

He nodded, "I know. I really care about you April, I've never met anyone like you before."

I could feel my cheeks getting hot, "I care about you too."

Our eyes locked and my heart beat quickened. He took my face in his hands and leant in slowly. I thought he was going to kiss me. In that moment, I realised that I actually wanted him to kiss me. I wanted him to take me away to that place where I didn't think about anything or anyone else. He gently kissed me on the forehead. That one kiss was so much more meaningful than any steamy kiss. I could feel how much he truly cared about me and I felt a tiny flutter, not in my stomach but in my heart.

When he pulled away and looked into my eyes, I thought I saw a flash of pain. Was he suffering from something in the same way that I was? Was I his security blanket?

"Thank you" I whispered.

"For what?"

"Being you."

He smiled, "You're only as good as the company you keep. It's getting late, I better go."

I nodded and helped him collect his things together whilst he rang for a taxi.

When it arrived, I walked him to the door, "See you in the morning?" I asked.

"Yep, bright and early."

I watched as he got into the taxi and waved to him as it drove off.

I went to bed feeling better but even more confused. I definitely had some sort of feelings for Lukas but my heart was still craving Isaac and it was putting up one hell of a fight.

I dreamt about him again that night. I dreamt that we were at the shop but this time he was with another woman. This time he spoke to me. He told me that he had moved on and was happy with his new girlfriend. I don't know what my subconscious was trying to tell me but I had a feeling that some part of me had started to fight for Lukas too.

Chapter Twelve

When I walked to class the next day, I groaned when I saw Hollie standing outside the entrance to the building. Thinking about both Lukas and Isaac had made me forget about my argument with her. As I approached her, I considered turning back around but I knew that I wouldn't be able to avoid her forever, not through lack of trying on my part. I took my earphones out and prepared myself to get an ear bashing. She was smiling at me, which made me suspicious straight away. She pounced on me when I got close enough.

"Can we talk?"

Talk or throw a drink in my face?

"Good morning to you too" I said sarcastically, not looking forward to what she wanted to 'talk' about.

She rolled her eyes, "Good morning April, now can we talk?"

"Well that depends. I thought we were talking on Saturday night but then you threw a drink in my face."

She looked around us at the people walking past and then gestured towards the bench directly opposite us, "Can we sit down for a minute?"

I shrugged, "Okay but my lecture starts in five minutes."

We walked over to the bench and with each step, I was regretting my decision not to turn and run in the opposite direction when I had the chance.

"I want to apologise for my behaviour the other night" she said.

Miracles really do happen.

"I'm sorry, what? Did I just hear you right?"

"Yes, you did. I also want you to know that I've never apologised to anybody in my entire life. So you know that when I say it, I mean it."

Who are you and what have you done with Hollie?

I nodded at her, completely shocked.

"I will pay for a new shirt seeing as though I ruined the one that you were wearing. So if you just tell me how much it was, I'll get the money to you straight away."

Then she looked at me, waiting for me to speak.

"Um...okay...thanks?" It came out as more of a question.

"Look, I know you might not believe me or accept my apology but I'm being honest with you. I needed to hear the truth and I respect you for having the balls to be the one to tell me. Nobody has ever said those things to my face which is why I reacted the way that I did. But everything you said was true."

Call me naive but I was actually buying it. "I accept your apology."

"You do?"

I nodded, "Yeah, I do. I'm not accepting the way that you behaved but I wasn't proud of how I acted either. I'm sorry if I was a little harsh, I shouldn't have called you a whore."

"Yes, you should have."

"I should have?"

"Yeah, I was acting like one so I should be called out on it. I need more people like you in my life."

I accept your apology but don't push it.

"I'm also sorry about putting the moves on your friend, I'll apologise to him too. I get it, he doesn't like me because he's into you. I'm not used to getting rejected that's all."

"We're just friends but you really shouldn't go around touching people like that."

"I know. That's not usually the response I get, let me tell you. And whilst we're calling each other out on our bullshit, open your eyes, he's totally into you."

"Like I said, we're just friends."

She watched me closely, "Deny, deny, deny. Trust me, I get it. For the record, I think you two make a nice couple."

I shrugged.

"Unless you're into somebody else?"

My defences came up so quick, they nearly hit both of us in the face.

"No" I shot back, a little too loud.

Why don't you answer a little faster and louder next time? Maybe Isaac will hear your protests all the way from his office.

"It's okay if you are. It's better to deal with your feelings, trust me I know."

"I don't know what you're talking about."

"Sure you don't. You're a good person, I'm sure you'll get everything you want in the end."

I really doubt that I'll get my happy ever after with my personal tutor but thanks for the optimism.

I stood up, "I'd better go in, the lecture will be starting."

"I hope we can be friends one day, April." I looked her in the eyes and could tell that she was being genuine.

"Maybe. Thanks for apologising, I know it must have been difficult for you."

She shrugged, "Easier than I thought it would be."

Hollie's words echoed through my mind for the next hour. I was pleasantly surprised that she apologised but worried about her comments about being into somebody else and 'dealing with my feelings'. There was no way that she could know anything about me and Isaac. Unless it was blatantly obvious on the day of the tutor meeting that we had feelings for each other. I thought that I had disguised it well but perhaps not.

"We don't have to worry about Hollie anymore." I told Lukas as we left class.

"Have you spoken to her?" I nodded. "Is that why you looked like you had a million things running through your mind during that lecture?"

"Yeah, it was strange. She actually apologised."

His eyes widened in shock, "Wow, I didn't think she knew what an apology was."

"Exactly. She apologised for everything and even offered to pay for my ruined shirt."

"What's she up to?"

"That's what's strange about it...I don't think she's up to anything. I think she meant it. She admitted that she was out of order and hopes that we can be friends one day."

"I'm speechless..."

"I think it was a wake-up call for her."

"Maybe."

"The proof is in the pudding I guess."

He smiled, "Speaking of puddings, can I take you to dinner tonight?"

"Oh...um...yeah" I nodded.

"We can try that awesome Chinese restaurant that I was telling you about. I'll pick you up around eight?"

"Sounds good. You've got to promise me something though..."

He looked at me questioningly, "What?"

"Promise that you won't wear your onesie."

He laughed, "I promise."

***

"You promised!"

He grinned from ear to ear, "I promised to not wear my onesie. I'm not wearing my onesie."

"No, you're not..." I replied whilst staring at the tartan kilt.

"Don't you like it? I'm very proud of it you know."

I tried my best to keep a straight face, "I like it. Are you at least wearing something underneath it?"

"Well you might find out later if you're lucky" he winked and I couldn't help but laugh.

"Or if there's a sudden gust of wind on our way over there?"

"Or that. I know which one I'd prefer" his eyes twinkled at me as I playfully swatted him on the arm.

"Come on, let's go and show your sexy legs off."

***

He was right, the food was amazing. I was that full, I was almost tempted to undo the top button of my jeans...almost. Instead, I slouched in my chair and sipped my third glass of wine. It was really starting to kick in now.

I groaned, "I can't bear to look at anymore food."

He chuckled before throwing his napkin down in defeat, "I'm stuffed. Shall we get the rest to take away?"

"What, like a doggy bag?"

He laughed, "Like a doggy bag except it's for humans and it's in a box, not a bag. So not really."

I rolled my eyes, "How do you know about these awesome places?"

"I do know things."

"Well yeah, but you've only been in Manchester for a few weeks."

"Okay what I should have said is, I do know a bunch of people."

I stuck my tongue out at him, "Mr Popular. It's who you know and not what you know, eh?"

"Yet there's nobody else I'd rather be with."

I blushed and quickly tried to shake it off, "Stop it, you're making me blush. Actually no, carry on..."

I laughed but he took it seriously, "You look absolutely stunning this evening."

"Well thank you, you don't look too bad yourself...even in a skirt."

"For the hundredth time, it's not a skirt."

"It's a skirt."

The skirt conversation lasted for another ten minutes before we decided to order another bottle of wine. Lukas insisted that it was his treat. I was already pretty drunk and knew that it wasn't the best idea but what's the worst that could happen?

"Are you trying to get me drunk?"

He thought about it before answering, "No. Although last time you were drunk, you kissed me. So it wouldn't be a bad thing."

I laughed, "I don't have to be drunk to kiss you."

His face turned serious, "You don't?"

I shook my head.

He looked around the restaurant, "In that case, where's the waiter? I'm going to cancel the bottle of wine."

I scowled at him and he laughed, his dark eyes twinkling.

By the time I had finished my fourth glass, we were both pretty wasted. We were having fun, playing our favourite game where we guessed the background stories of the people around us.

"What about that guy?" I pointed towards a man who was sat with a woman at a table not too far from us. They were both wearing suits and looked like business types.

"How many times have I told you to stop pointing? You're going to get us into trouble."

"Trouble schmouble. Trouble follows me around anyway...well not so much anymore. It used to follow me around all of the time and steal me away but now it just ignores me."

April, stop talking.

He laughed, "You've lost me. What are you even talking about?"

I shrugged. I couldn't exactly tell him that I was talking about Isaac. I should stop drinking.

"So, what's their story?" I asked.

Lukas stroked his chin playfully which made me giggle, "His name is Roberto, he's forty and he runs his own business."

"That's a given with the suit. What kind of business?"

"He's in the porn industry."

I burst out laughing, "What's his stage name?"

"The Italian Stallion"

I looked over at him, "He's not Italian."

"Um...his name is Roberto, of course he's Italian."

"Okay, tell me more about *Roberto*."

"He's hiding a secret."

"Oh, this is getting good" I replied.

"He's completely crazy about his business partner. Can you see the way that he's looking at her?" I looked over but they both looked kind of bored. When I looked back at Lukas, he was looking at me with such intensity that it made my head spin. He carried on with his story whilst keeping his eyes fixed on mine the whole time.

"It's difficult though because they're friends, good friends. He doesn't want anything to ruin their friendship but he doesn't want to lose the opportunity to be with her. He knows that they can make each other happy. He's too scared to talk to her about it though so for now he's watching her every move from across the table, hoping that one day he can call her his."

Okay, this really wasn't how our games usually went down. His words were loaded and I could see the raw emotion in his eyes. I cleared my throat, "Maybe she's scared too."

He nodded, "I think she is."

"She really cares about him but she doesn't know if she's ready to give herself to him right now."

"He can wait, she's worth it."

I smiled and closed my eyes for a moment, wondering what I had done to deserve his affections. I opened them when he spoke.

"When they're together, he feels invincible."

"Like nothing else matters" I added.

"Except for them two."

I nodded. Looks like we were on the same page after all.

"Roberto is awesome" I announced and we both laughed.

"Come on, let's ask for a doggy bag and get out of here" I said.

"You mean a human box?" he replied, grinning.

***

Although we didn't talk much on the taxi ride home, he held my hand and didn't let go until we pulled up outside my house. "Wait here" he said before he jumped out and walked around my side to open the door for me.

Who said chivalry was dead?

95

"Thank you" I said, grinning.

"Thank *you* for another amazing evening" he replied.

I didn't want the night to end and felt disappointed that he was about to leave. I didn't know if it was down to the alcohol or my true feelings coming out. Maybe it was a little bit of both.

"Do you want to come in for a drink?" I asked.

He smiled, "I'd like that."

"I'll go and let us in" I said, before walking down the path to my front door. I heard Lukas pay the taxi driver before jogging back to me.

"Be careful jogging like that, the neighbours will get an eye full."

He laughed, "That's the only reason you've invited me in, isn't it? To find out what's underneath my kilt?"

I grinned and held my hands up, "Busted."

I held the door open for him and then closed it behind us, "Do you want a coffee?" I asked as he followed me into the living room.

"No thanks, I'd never get to sleep if I had caffeine at this time."

I looked at my watch and saw that it was almost midnight, "I didn't realise it was that late. Water then?"

"That's better, thanks."

"Sit down, I'll bring it to you." He sat down on the sofa as I headed towards the kitchen. I took my heels off on the way, "Wow, that feels so good."

I heard him laugh, "Sounds like you're having fun back there."

"Oh, um, sorry. I've just taken my heels off" I shouted as I filled two glasses with tap water before making my way back to him. "Honestly, I can't begin to tell you how good it feels. You should try it some time, we can match the heels to your skirt."

He took a sip of his water and nearly choked on it, "I'm going to have to take it off if you keep calling it a skirt."

"Skirt skirt skirt, la la la." That last glass of wine was really taking effect. "I'm hot" I said, fanning myself which had no effect whatsoever. "Do you want to sit outside?"

"Lead the way."

I walked over to the patio doors which lead into the back garden. It was only small but I liked it. It had a patio area with a table and chairs and a little grass area. I was looking forward to having BBQ's when the weather got nicer. At least tonight was dry and not too cold. Lukas walked over to one of the chairs but I went and laid down on the grass, looking up at the sky. It had been unusually clear these past few days so I stared at the sky and tried to join all of the stars together like a giant dot to dot game. My head was spinning even worse lying down but I didn't have the energy to get back up. Lukas stood next to me, looking down.

"Is it nice down there?"

"If you come a little closer, I'll be able to see right up your kilt."

He laughed and lay down next to me.

"Do you do this a lot?"

"What, look up people's kilts? Can't say that I do."

"You're on fire tonight."

I grinned, "Right? I'm glad you've noticed."

"Do you lie outside a lot?"

"Me and my best friend used to do it all of the time when we were at college. This is my first time doing it here though."

"Well I'm glad your first time is with me."

I laughed.

"So we've christened the garden, now what?"

Our definitions of christening something were slightly off.

"Now we relax."

"I can do that."

We laid there for a good ten minutes in silence. It was peaceful. It wasn't awkward and I didn't feel the need to blurt out something stupid. I felt safe with him lying next to me. I thought about our conversation in the restaurant. He had said that he was crazy about me and hoped that one day we could be together. I began questioning what exactly I was waiting for. Yes, I had feelings for Isaac but what if they never went away? How long was I willing to wait? Lukas was the one who was here by my side, not Isaac.

"Lukas?"

"Yes?"

"Kiss me."

He sat up at lightning speed, "What? Are you sure?"

I thought for a moment. This is what I wanted but was I being selfish getting involved with him when my dreams were haunted by another man? Or was I being selfish on my own happiness by not allowing myself to fall for him because I was consumed by a man that I could never have?

"I'm sure" I replied.

He slowly leant forward and brushed a strand of hair away from my face. His lips were inches away from mine and his eyes were full of emotion. I was suddenly overwhelmed by it all. There was no going back after this kiss, we both knew what it meant. It was about to alter our future. My heart started beating faster as I could feel the warmth of his breath.

I jumped when my phone started ringing in my bag. It was one of those cross body bags and I hadn't taken it off. I backed away from him and instantly saw the disappointment in his eyes.

"Sorry, I'll turn it off." I reached in for my phone and my stomach did a somersault when I saw Isaac's name flashing across my screen. I stared at it in shock. Why was he calling me? My need to know outweighed any other rational thought.

"Sorry, I need to take this." I told Lukas as I stood up and walked back inside the house. I knew that it was shitty of me to leave him alone in the garden after ruining the perfect moment, but all I cared about was hearing Isaac's voice. I pressed the accept button and heard loud music playing. When he didn't say anything after a few seconds, I started to think that he must have called me by accident. But that's when I heard him speak.

"Hello? April?"

I didn't know what to say so I kept quiet. I walked into the bedroom and sat down on the edge of my bed. The music grew quieter until eventually, all that I could hear was his breathing. For some reason, I found it comforting.

"Are you there? Please say something."

"I'm here" I whispered.

"We need to talk" he said bluntly.

"*We* don't need to do anything, I'm busy" I shot back.

"Doing what?"

"I've got guests."

"At this time?"

"Yes, at this time. I'm not a child, I can do whatever the hell I like." I stood up and began pacing around the room.

"Wait...have you been drinking?"

"It's none of your goddamn business."

"Are you drunk? On a week night?" He sounded shocked.

"So what if I am, it's quite obvious that you are. Stop being such a hypocrite."

"I'm not drunk" he replied.

I snorted, "Okay then neither am I."

"But I've not got classes all day tomorrow."

99

"That's right, you haven't got any classes because you *work* for the university."

"I'm well aware of that."

"Yeah well that makes two of us."

"Fuck!" he shouted, making me jump. "I thought I could do this but I can't. You're driving me fucking crazy."

"I'm driving you crazy? I'm not doing anything!"

"Exactly, that's my fucking point."

I had to take some deep breaths to calm myself down. How dare he say that I was driving him crazy when he was the one running hot and cold.

"You should watch your language around your students, surely that's in your contract."

He laughed but still sounded angry, "Yeah well you should watch your smart mouth before it gets you into trouble. You're making all of this very difficult."

I didn't think it was possible but my heart started beating even faster. I was pretty sure that it was going to explode any minute now.

"Isaac...what is this about? Why did you call me?"

"I needed closure but obviously..."

The knock on my bedroom door distracted me from what he was saying. I looked up to see Lukas and panicked. I wondered how long he had been standing there. Had he heard anything? I let the phone drop to my side. "I'll just be one more minute." He nodded before walking away.

"I need to go" I told Isaac.

"Who were you talking to?"

"Nobody, I have to go."

"Wait, did you hear what I just said?"

"Yes, you need closure. Well I hope you've got it."

"April...wait..."

I hung up and turned the power off. I couldn't take any more phone calls tonight. I was a ticking time bomb of emotion ready to explode. I was frustrated at how happy I felt just from hearing his voice. Isaac was like a drug. I knew he wasn't good for me but I was addicted to him. I needed my fix however I could get it. Good or bad was better than nothing at all. But now I was left to deal with the come down. It physically hurt me when I thought about him wanting closure. I also felt horrible for leaving Lukas in the garden alone like that, it was completely selfish of me. I was angry at Isaac for messing up a perfectly good evening for me and Lukas. I took a couple of deep breaths before walking into the living room, not wanting to leave Lukas on his own any longer.

"I'm really sorry about that" I said to him.

He gave me a sad smile which made me feel even worse. "I think I should go, it's getting late. I didn't want to leave without saying goodbye."

I nodded, "Thanks, maybe we can do something another night?"

"Maybe." He stood up and gave me a small hug. It wasn't the usual bear hug that I was used to getting from him.

"See you tomorrow" he said as he left. I watched him walk down the street in his kilt, no sign of a taxi anywhere.

As soon as I locked the door, the waterworks started. I was sick of feeling this way. I deserved to be happy and couldn't keep jeopardising my future happiness.

Isaac could take his closure and stick it where the sun doesn't shine.

It was time for me to take control.

Chapter Thirteen

When my alarm clock went off the next morning, I instantly regretted drinking so much. My head pounded and my throat felt like sandpaper. I crawled to the bathroom and pulled myself up into the bath tub. I couldn't bear to stand up whilst I had a shower so I ran myself a bath instead. Why did I let myself drink so much on a school night?

My mind wandered back to the events of last night. I desperately wanted to see Lukas to check that he was okay. It had been wrong of me to drop everything and go running off to answer Isaac's phone call. The phone call where he had said that he wanted closure. He had sounded completely different, not the intelligent, funny man that I thought I knew.

I jumped out of the bath and made it to the toilet just in time to throw up. When I was positive that I wasn't going to be sick anymore, I stood up carefully and dried myself. After throwing some clothes on, I went to get my phone from the bedroom. I wanted to check in case Lukas had tried to ring me. I switched it on and it buzzed immediately. 3 missed calls and a voicemail from Isaac. Two of the calls were from late last night but the third one was from this morning, around an hour ago. I didn't want to listen to it. I wanted to be strong enough to delete it without listening but that wasn't going to happen anytime soon. I nervously dialled voicemail and listened to his message -

"April, I just want to say sorry for my behaviour last night. It was completely inappropriate and unprofessional of me. I shouldn't have called you. I drank way too much and wasn't being myself. I'm sorry if I upset you, I can assure you that it won't happen again. Take care."

Take care? I shook my head and angrily threw my phone across the bedroom. His mood swings were giving me whiplash. He sounded so professional and rehearsed, nothing like the Isaac that I spoke to last night. At least he had assured me that it wasn't going to happen again. Now that he had closure, I could get mine. It was time to move on.

After putting some make up on, I grabbed my bag and headed out. I rang Lukas on my walk over to the lecture. Just when it was about to go to voicemail, he answered.

"Hey." He didn't sound like his usual self.

"Morning, how are you?" I asked.

"Not bad, you?"

"Same, hung over."

"So what's up? Are you coming in today?" he asked.

"Yeah, I'm walking up now. I just wanted to apologise again about getting interrupted last night. I didn't know if I'd get chance to talk to you in the lecture."

"You don't need to apologise."

"Yes I do, I left you in the garden on your own. I'm sorry."

"I'm over it."

"I want to make it up to you."

"I'm listening..."

"I want to cook you dinner. You keep taking me to all of these wonderful restaurants so I want to repay the favour."

He laughed, "You don't have to do that."

"I know I don't have to but I want to."

"Can I trust your cooking?"

"There's only one way to find out."

"When are you thinking?"

"Tonight?"

He went quiet for a moment. "Two nights in a row...are you sure? The neighbours will start talking."

"They're already talking about you and your dress sense."

"Don't pretend you don't love it."

I laughed, "I'm almost here so I'll see you in a few minutes."

I walked into the lecture feeling a lot happier. I was looking forward to spending the evening with Lukas, this time without any interruptions.

***

The day went by quickly and even though I felt hung over, Lukas did a good job of distracting me. He was his usual happy self and I was grateful that he didn't mention the phone call. I didn't want to lie to him if he asked who I had been talking to.

Although we were going to see each other in a few hours, he walked me home at the end of the day. The air felt charged between us and I even felt a little bit nervous. When we got onto my street, he took my hand in his and held it until we got to my front door.

"I'm looking forward to later" he said.

I smiled warmly, "Me too, I hope you like my cooking."

"I'm sure that I will but even if I didn't, I wouldn't care. I just want your company."

I laughed, "In that case, I'll order pizza."

"Whatever you make will be delicious."

I loved the way that he looked at me with so much affection. He didn't try and hide his emotions, he let them show through his eyes.

"See you later" he whispered in my ear whilst giving me a hug.

"I can't wait" I replied before watching him walk away.

Once I got inside, I squealed with excitement. This was my chance at happiness.

***

I left the lasagne cooking in the oven whilst I took a quick shower and chose what to wear.

Whilst I was getting changed into one of my favourite dresses, my phone rang. My breath caught and my stomach flipped, I hoped to god that it wasn't Isaac. Even though I wouldn't answer it this time, I didn't want to think about him at all tonight. I picked it up off the bed and felt relieved when I saw that it was Katie. I answered it straight away with a huge smile on my face.

"Hey Kitty."

"What's happened?"

"You really need to start working on your greetings..."

"Hello, what's happened?"

I laughed, "Can you be a little more specific?"

"You sound really happy."

"I'm just in a good mood for a change."

"Oh my god, has something happened with Isaac?"

I groaned in response.

"I'll take that as a no then" she replied.

"My good mood has got nothing to do with him."

"So who then?"

"Katie, my happiness doesn't depend on a man."

"Yeah right, like my happiness doesn't depend on how many times Jamie wakes me up during the night."

I rolled my eyes.

"Where was this attitude when you spent weeks moping over Isaac?" she asked.

"Look, we're not talking about him anymore."

"We're not?"

"Nope, I'm having a fresh start. I'm just putting you on speaker phone whilst I finish getting ready." I put the phone back down on the bed before choosing which earrings to wear.

"Getting ready for what?"

"Lukas is coming round, I'm cooking for us."

"Oh my god...you're totally going to sleep with him."

"I'm totally not."

"Well why are you cooking dinner for him then?"

"I don't know how it works at your house but I'm cooking because we need to eat."

"Keep going..."

"That's it. No ulterior motive."

"Hmmm, maybe that's where I'm going wrong. Do you think if I start cooking then Ian might sleep with me?"

I laughed, "Maybe you could just talk to him about it."

"I shouldn't have to, he should want to have sex with me. I feel like a horny little teenager."

"You *are* a horny little teenager."

"I'm not little, I'm taller than you."

After putting my jewellery on, I carried the phone into the kitchen to check on the lasagne. It wasn't burning so that was a good start.

"So what's been happening? You're starting to forget about me" she asked.

I laughed, "No I'm not, I've just been busy."

"That's how it all starts."

"Shut up."

"See."

I laughed, "I really like Lukas."

"I knew it! Now you can stop telling me that you're just friends."

"Well I don't want to ruin our friendship, I want to take things slow. We went out for dinner last night and sort of admitted that we've got feelings for each other."

"What did he say?"

"We were playing a game, it's hard to explain."

"A game? Like spin the bottle?"

"No, I'm not thirteen anymore."

"Well what kind of game?"

"I guess it was like role-playing."

"What?" she shouted down the phone, nearly deafening me. "I didn't know you were into role-playing, you dirty girl!"

"No, not like that. It wasn't dirty. I've not got time to go into it now but we're on the same page."

"So what made you change your mind about Isaac?"

Was she always going to bring him into it?

"He rang me last night for *closure*." I hated that word.

"Fuck me, I wasn't expecting that."

"He was drunk, we both were."

I heard her squeal, "I am totally air high-fiving the shit out of you right now."

"Why?" I said, completely confused.

"Because you've made a sex god fall in love with you."

I rolled my eyes, "And how do you figure that one out?"

"You only drunk dial someone if you're in love with them. It's a well known fact. Alcohol makes the truth come out."

"Yeah well the truth did come out, he said he wanted closure."

"Bullshit. You gave him closure at the football game. He rang you because he still wants you. He could have been out having fun and getting laid but instead he called you. He's got it bad."

"No..."

"Yes. He's totally in love with your ass."

"Will you stop saying that?"

"Will you start believing it?"

I felt light headed so sat down on the sofa. Of course he wasn't in love with me. She'll be saying that he wants to marry me next. The butterflies in my stomach went crazy as the words that I had forbidden myself to remember over the past few weeks came flooding back, 'I'm going to marry that girl one day'.

"I need to stop talking to you. You really mess with my head."

"You should be blaming Isaac, not me."

"I've got to go, Lukas will be here any minute now."

"Have fun."

I groaned when I came off the phone to Katie. I had been determined not to think about Isaac but now I couldn't think about anything else but him. No, she had it all wrong. He wasn't in love with me. If he was, he wouldn't have ignored me at the shop or told me that he needed closure. At least, that's what I kept telling myself for the next ten minutes until Lukas arrived.

His eyes roamed the full length of my body, "You look lovely."

"Oh, this old thing?" I said, trying not to blush.

He laughed, "The food smells wonderful."

"I hope it tastes as good as it smells. You do like lasagne, right?"

"No, I'm allergic."

"What?" I panicked.

"I'm joking, it's my favourite."

I playfully poked him in the chest and he reached around and pulled me into a big hug. I instantly felt better as I smiled up at him. I wasn't going to let anything or anyone ruin our evening.

***

"That was delicious, thank you" he said as we made our way over to the sofa with our glasses of wine.

"I'm glad you liked it."

"Now that I know you can cook, I'm going to be here a lot more."

"Maybe that was my plan all along."

"Things are slowly starting to add up."

I laughed as I sat down next to him, our thighs touching. The air around us felt charged.

"What would you like to do now?" I asked.

"Whatever you want is fine with me."

For the first time this evening, I felt nervous. What I really wanted to do was kiss him. His eyes were fixed on mine as the corners of his mouth turned up into a small smile. I watched him carefully as he leant in closer, his lips hovering close to mine as his hand rested on the small of my back. Just when I thought he was going to kiss me, he whispered "You left me waiting last night, now it's my turn." He pulled away and I could see the playfulness in his eyes. If I really wanted to, I knew that I could kiss him there and then but I decided to play along with his game. After all, wasn't the anticipation of the kiss meant to better than the actual kiss?

"I hate you" I told him.

"No you don't."

"No, I don't."

He laughed, "Do you want to watch a movie?"

"Sounds good, you can choose this time."

***

"April, wake up" I heard Lukas whisper. I opened my eyes to see him smiling down at me. "You fell asleep. I didn't want to wake you but it's getting late."

"How long have I been asleep?"

"About an hour, the movie finished half an hour ago."

"I'm sorry, I'm a pretty crappy host."

"No you're not, I quite like watching you sleep. Oh wait, that sounded creepy. I didn't mean it like that."

I laughed as I stretched, "You totally meant it like that."

He grinned, "Busted."

"Was the end of the movie good?"

"Nah."

I raised my eyebrow, "It was good, wasn't it?"

"Totally awesome, you missed the best part."

We both laughed as we stood up.

"I've had an awesome evening so thank you" he said. His grin made my heart happy.

"Me too."

"I'll see you tomorrow, gorgeous."

"I like the sound of that."

"What, me calling you gorgeous?"

I blushed, "That too. See you tomorrow."

He pulled me into a hug before waving and jogging down the

street.

Chapter Fourteen

The next morning, I got ready with a huge smile on my face. My dreams had been free from Isaac and I was looking forward to seeing Lukas again. When I turned my phone on, I had three missed calls from Katie. I rang her straight back.

"Is everything okay?" I asked.

"Now who needs to work on their greetings?"

"Has something happened?"

"You tell me" she said.

I sighed, "Katie, what's up?"

"Nothing, I'm just checking how it went with Lukey boy."

"Please don't call him that."

She laughed, "Well?"

"We had a nice evening."

"Sounds exciting" she said, sarcastically. "At least you didn't poison him."

"I love you too, best friend."

"Did you sleep with him?"

"No."

"So do you like this guy or what?"

"Of course I like him."

"No I mean, *like him* like him."

I put my coat on and grabbed my bag before heading out.

"Thanks for clearing that up. Yes, *I like him* like him" I said as I opened the front door.

I nearly had a heart attack when I saw Lukas standing there with a big grin on his face. "I hope you're talking about me."

I took a deep breath and placed my hand over my heart, "You scared me."

"I'm sorry, I was about to knock when you opened the door."

I could hear Katie chirping down the phone, "Is that him?"

"Yes, Lukas is here" I told her.

"Tell him I said hello."

I rolled my eyes, "Katie says hello."

He laughed, "Hey Katie."

"Now tell him that if he ever hurts you, I will cut off his..."

"I'll call you later, bye!"

I shook my head as I put my phone in my bag and then locked the door. "Sorry about that. Is everything okay?" I asked.

"Everything's great, I just wanted to walk you to class."

I grinned as he held out his hand for mine.

We walked the whole way to class holding hands which felt a little strange at first when we saw people that we knew but it also made me feel giddy. However, when we reached campus, I couldn't help but feel nervous in case we saw Isaac. I couldn't deal with him right now. Luckily, the coast was clear.

We walked into the seminar to the sounds of wolf whistles and I heard Lucy shout something which sounded like 'about time'. Lukas laughed and kissed my hand dramatically. I hated being the centre of attention.

"Stop encouraging them" I told him, blushing. It was only a small class so all eyes were on us and most people were grinning. Most people except for Hollie. She was trying to get my attention using her eyes and nodded towards something behind me. I knew what was happening, she was warning me but it was too late. I heard somebody clear their throat. I turned around to see Isaac glaring at Lukas. His eyes were bright and intimidating. Jeez, he could have at least tried to mask it.

"Mr Roberts, please can I have a word?" His voice was sharp and blunt.

I started to panic. Why did he want to speak to Lukas?

Lukas shrugged, "Sure". He looked down at me, "See you in a minute."

I nodded and then watched as he walked out of the room behind Isaac.

I was left standing there, staring at the door. Hollie stood up and walked over to me, "Come and sit down next to me."

I did as she asked but all I really wanted to do was go outside and listen to whatever Isaac had to say. My mind went into overdrive. Surely Isaac wouldn't tell Lukas about the night of the mixer. I felt a pang of guilt that Isaac had to witness our little performance. Why of all the days did he have to be in our class today? I should probably go and check that he's not beating the crap out of Lukas.

"I tried to warn you but the others wouldn't shut up" Hollie whispered. What does she know? Why did she think it was necessary to warn me that Isaac was in the room?

"Isaac looked pretty pissed off" she added.

So I wasn't the only one to notice.

"I didn't notice" I lied.

She smiled, "I'm sure you didn't. Hmmm, I wonder what could have caused him to be so pissed off."

The door opened and Lukas came back in looking confused. He sat down in the closest chair to him which was on the opposite side of the room to me. I tried to catch his attention but he was staring at the front of the classroom, looking deep in thought. This wasn't looking good.

The next fifty minutes was torture. Time passed slowly and I couldn't concentrate on anything other than the way Isaac had looked and the way that Lukas was looking now. As soon as class was dismissed, I rushed over to Lukas.

"Hey" I said.

He smiled in response.

"Are you okay?" I asked as we made our way out of the classroom.

"Yeah, I'm fine."

"I'm sorry for not saving you a seat, Hollie dragged me over to sit with her."

"It's okay."

"You seem weird."

"Do I? Sorry."

"What did Isaac talk to you about?"

He shook his head, "It was strange. He started off by telling me about somebody who he knows in Scotland who might be able to get me some work experience."

"Oh. That sounds good."

"Well yeah but then he gave me a lecture about working hard and not getting distracted."

"What did he mean, not getting distracted?"

I knew full well what he meant.

"By drinking and partying. I think the dude might be gay, he was pretty adamant that I don't date."

I had to bite my lip to stop myself from laughing. Isaac is a lot of things but he is definitely not gay.

"He asked me if you were my girlfriend."

Okay, I didn't feel like laughing any more.

"What did you say?"

"I told him that we're good friends."

Why did I feel relieved? Did I still care what Isaac thought? The answer was obvious.

"He spoke very highly of you. He said that you're different from other girls. He doesn't want you to get distracted from your work either."

Yeah, I'm sure that's all he's worried about. I'm sure it has nothing to do with the fact that he doesn't want me to date another man.

"He said that he's going to monitor us both closely to check that our grades don't drop."

I could feel myself getting angry. Who on earth does he think that he is? I took several deep breaths and tried to keep my voice level, "Please just ignore him. He has no right to tell us what to do."

He wrapped his arm around me, "I know."

I put on a fake smile, "I just need to nip to the finance office. I'll catch you later, okay?"

"Do you want me to come with you?"

"No, it's okay. It'll be boring." I waved and walked off in the direction of the finance office, which happened to be in the same building as Isaac's office.

I was so angry at him. How dare he try and warn Lukas off like that. He had overstepped the mark this time. He told me that he needed closure so why was he getting involved in my relationships? The more I thought about it, the more worked up I got.

When I got to the Synergy building, I took the lift up to the third floor and stormed up to his office door. I regretted knocking so hard as it hurt my knuckles.

"Come in" he shouted.

I went inside and stopped in front of his desk. He didn't look surprised to see me, if anything he looked amused.

"How dare you try and warn Lukas to stay away from me."

He took his glasses off and leaned back in his leather chair.

"Lovely to see you as always, April."

I felt a rush of excitement when he said my name.

"I wish that I could say the same about you" I replied.

The corners of his mouth turned up as he looked me up and down. I felt like I was on display.

"Stop looking at me like that."

"Like what?"

I rolled my eyes, "Like I'm a piece of meat."

His smile grew wider. I began to pace up and down his office, "Isaac, you can't do this. This is messed up."

"I'll tell you what's messed up, watching you play happy families with Lukas."

"Who said anything about playing?"

"It's obvious. Look me in the eyes and tell me that you don't have any feelings for me."

"Shhhh, keep your goddamn voice down." I was paranoid in case somebody walked past and heard our conversation.

"Answer the question" he said.

"It doesn't matter if I have feelings for you."

"Of course it matters. As long as you have feelings for me, I'm not going anywhere."

I sighed, "I don't have feelings for you."

"You're a terrible liar."

"You're a terrible tutor."

"Again, terrible liar."

I growled to stop myself from screaming in frustration. I wanted to throw something at his head when he laughed at me.

I sat down and took a deep breath, "Please stop it."

He leant forward, "April, what's the deal with Lukas? You don't need to do this, you know. You don't need to be with him just to prove a point." His voice was soft now.

"I want to be with him."

His eyes burned into mine, "I don't think you know what you want."

I stood up, "I'm not doing this. I came here to tell you to stay away from Lukas."

"I'll stay away from him but I can't say the same about you."

"Well try your best."

"I always do."

I slammed the door behind me. God, that man knew how to push my buttons. I didn't know if my visit to him had been a help or a hindrance. As long as he stayed away from Lukas then I could deal with the rest. He was the most frustrating person that I had ever met. The funny thing was, he was turning me into a close second.

***

I wasn't in any other classes with Lukas for the rest of the day which was a good thing. I needed some time alone to get my head straight. I stayed in the library at dinner and text him to tell him that I was busy and would see him tomorrow. It usually took a whole day to recover from one of Isaac's mood swings.

When I got home, I rang Katie.

"What's going on?" she asked.

I sighed, "I give up."

"With?"

"Isaac saw me and Lukas holding hands, then warned him to

stay away from me."

"I told you, he's totally in love with you!"

"Stop squealing, that's really not helping."

"Sorry. What did Lukas say about it?"

"Nothing really, he was confused. Apparently, Isaac made out like he was concerned about our grades dropping."

"Well played."

"Please remember whose side you're on."

"Oh come on, didn't it make you feel good?"

"No, it made me feel worse."

"Explain..."

"I'm trying my hardest to have a normal relationship with a guy that I genuinely like. It doesn't help to know that Isaac still has feelings for me. I'd rather him move on and forget about me. It's like taking one step forwards and two steps back."

"You don't mean that."

I groaned.

"So what's the plan?" she asked.

"I went and told Isaac to leave Lukas alone."

"You did what?"

"I went and told Isaac to..."

"I heard you the first time, why did you do that?"

"Because he needs to give me some space. This morning, I was happy with Lukas but then he has to go and piss all over my bonfire."

"Is that some sort of innuendo?"

"Jesus Katie, no."

"Well I've got some good news that might cheer you up."

"What?" I asked, sounding unenthusiastic.

"I'm coming to see you next weekend!"

I squealed, "Oh my god!"

"See, I knew it would cheer you up! I need a little break and my mum's agreed to look after Jamie whilst Ian's at work."

"I can't wait to see you! I'm going to start counting down the days...no, the hours!"

Katie's news made my evening a lot better. I ran myself a bath and read one of my favourite books that always managed to make me smile. That night, instead of dreaming about Isaac, I dreamt about a hot tattooed guy at an underground fight club. Needless to say, I woke up with a huge smile on my face.

Chapter Fifteen

At least Isaac didn't show up in anymore of my classes or dreams that week. The news of Katie's visit had perked me up and I was feeling more like my old self. Lukas continued to walk me to class each morning and I was glad that Isaac's attempt at scaring him off had failed.

On Friday night, me and Lukas made our way over to his place. Dan was hosting a poker night and Lukas wanted to be there to keep an eye on the flat. I didn't blame him after hearing about some of the things Dan got up to when he was drunk. Lucy and some other people that I knew were going too and I was looking forward to seeing their flat for the first time.

When I walked into the living room, I was pleasantly surprised. It wasn't the unclean, smelly flat that I had expected. It was modern and clean and I had a feeling that this was down to Lukas, not Dan. It had a black and white colour scheme with wooden floors. The walls were painted white with all black furniture, including two comfy looking leather sofas. They were currently occupied by Lucy and some of her friends who I recognised from the football game. Lukas gave me a quick tour of the rest of the house, saving his bedroom until last.

"I think you need a bigger bed" I said whilst grinning at the king size in the middle of the room.

He laughed, "Don't worry, we can both fit in it."

"To sleep?" I asked.

"Of course."

I looked around, it was very minimalistic. No books, no photographs, no socks on the floor, nothing. It had fitted wardrobes with a matching desk and a flat screen attached to the wall but that was it.

I perched on the edge of his bed, "I like it."

"Well I like you" he said as he sat down next to me. I grinned and rested my hand on his thigh. He slowly moved my hair to one side before leaning down and peppering my neck with kisses. I closed my eyes and gripped his leg tighter.

"Does this mean that the wait is over?" I asked.

"Huh?" he murmured against my skin.

My hand travelled higher up his leg and he moaned at my touch. I suddenly wished that we were the only two people home. "You said that you were making me wait because I made you wait."

He positioned me so that I was straddling him. "We've both waited long enough" he said.

I nodded, suddenly aware of how heavy my breathing was. He kissed me hard and fast and I pressed my weight down on him, forcing his body to press against mine. I moaned in his mouth and when the kiss became more intense, I forced myself to pull away. I closed my eyes and took a deep breath, trying to compose myself. I stood up slowly.

"Um...poker...outside..."

He laughed, "That was your good luck kiss."

I grinned, "Well in that case, I need another one."

***

"Let the games begin, boys" Dan shouted as they made their way over to the table.

"And girls, sexist pig" I mumbled as I stood up from the sofa.

"Oh, are you getting a drink?" Lucy asked.

"No, I'm going to play poker. You heard Dan, they're starting."

"You're playing?" One of the other girls asked me, looking shocked. I should probably find out what her name is.

I nodded, "I'm guessing you're not?" I felt like asking her why she was even here.

"No, I just come to chill out and serve the drinks."

I snorted, "You're kidding right? You serve them drinks?"

She shrugged.

Way to play up to stereotypes.

"Well it's poker night and I've come to play poker, watch and learn ladies."

As I approached the table, Dan looked up, "I'll have a beer please, sweet cheeks."

I sat down next to Lukas, "Get your own beer, sweet cheeks. I'm here to play."

He laughed, "Good one."

"Seriously, what is wrong with you people? It's a poker night, I'm playing poker. Girls can play too so shut up and deal the cards."

He narrowed his eyes and then shrugged, "Well don't come crying to me when you lose all of your money."

"Oh don't worry, that's not going to happen" I replied.

I felt a hand on my leg and turned to see Lukas wearing a proud smile. I placed my hand on his until Dan dealt the cards. Then it was time to get down to business.

***

"You have got to be fucking kidding me" Dan said as I revealed my royal flush, beating his full house.

"Read 'em and weep boys, read 'em and weep" I said as I collected the cash from the middle of the table.

"Are you cheating?" Dan asked.

"No, I'm just shit hot at poker."

"How?"

"I'm naturally gifted, Daniel."

Lukas chuckled at the big grin on my face.

"Let's go again" Dan said.

An hour later, I had officially emptied all of their pockets and

Dan was trying to bet using household appliances. I told him that I had no interest in winning his kettle and microwave.

"Good game fellas, same time next week?" I asked.

The others laughed and shook their heads but Dan was in a mood.

"Fuck that. I'm going out, who's coming?"

The girls jumped up off the sofa and followed the guys outside.

"Do you want to?" Lukas asked.

"Hell yeah, I've got all of Dan's money to spend."

"You're awesome, do you know that?"

I grinned, "If I say no, will you carry on saying it?"

***

I woke up on Saturday afternoon feeling like I had been hit by a bus. I tried to sit up but my head felt too heavy. I was fully clothed and my hands were covered in stamps from different night clubs. I reached over to my bedside table to get a glass of water before downing it. When I tried to put it back, I missed the table and it fell to the floor. That's when I noticed the bucket next to my bed. I smiled, Lukas must have made sure that I got home safe last night.

I nearly had a heart attack when I heard footsteps followed by a knock on my bedroom door. Somebody was in the house. I panicked and looked for my phone until I heard Lukas's voice.

"April? Can I come in?"

I desperately tried to remember what had happened last night. Why was he here?

"Um...you can come in" I said, flattening my hair down.

He opened the door slowly and smiled when he saw me.

"Did you...? Did we...?"

"No, I slept on the sofa. I hope you don't mind, I wanted to be here to check that you were okay."

"I don't mind, thank you." I covered my face with my hands, "'I can't remember anything from last night. Did I do shots?"

"Understatement of the century. I tried stopping you but you wouldn't listen."

I shook my head, "Every time. I never learn."

"So I'm guessing that you don't remember singing *'We are the champions' by Queen* on karaoke...twice?"

I groaned, "Not at all."

"You were good. You dedicated it to Dan both times."

"Why?"

"Because you beat him at poker and he was being a big girl about it."

I grinned, "I remember beating him but that's about it."

"Don't worry, I'm pretty sure somebody recorded you singing. You really got in role."

"Fantastic. I need to stop drinking."

"At least you had fun."

I laughed, "Did I?"

"We both did."

"You didn't have to sleep on the sofa you know, this bed is pretty roomy."

"That's what you kept saying last night."

"Oh god, did I do anything...inappropriate?"

He laughed.

"So that's a yes. I'm so sorry, was it bad?"

"It was good, apart from when you tried to strip me in the taxi on the way home. But we were both wasted and I didn't want us to do something that we might have ended up regretting so I stayed on the sofa."

"Well thank you and I'm sorry."

"You've got nothing to be sorry about."

Lukas stayed at my house for most of Saturday. We ordered take away and watched the '*Die Hard*' movies back to back. I felt too ill to do anything more than hold hands but that was good enough for me. Just having him there made me feel better.

The house felt quiet after he left but I fell asleep almost instantly.

Sunday was spent doing housework and catching up on coursework followed by a much needed early night.

Chapter Sixteen

"I think I'm in love" Dan announced as we watched the cheerleaders at the midweek football game.

"With what? Her ass?" I asked.

He scowled at me, "No...her rack."

He found this hilarious and went to high five Lukas. "Don't leave me hanging, bro..."

Lukas just shook his head in response and I giggled.

"How are things with you and Hollie?" Lucy asked him. There was a hint of jealousy in her voice which I could tell she was trying hard to mask. It confirmed my suspicions that she had some sort of feelings for Dan. In a way, I was glad that he was such a jerk and went after girls like Hollie because Lucy was too nice for him.

"Fucking amazeballs. Three times a night, five nights a week."

I rolled my eyes then nudged Lucy as the football players ran onto the pitch. It seemed to cheer her up a little bit.

Hollie made her way over to us once she finished cheering and it didn't take Dan very long to shove his tongue down her throat. They took PDA to a whole new level, it was like watching a live porn show.

I glanced at Lucy and noticed the grimace on her face, "Will you two cut it out?" I asked.

Hollie laughed and pulled away from him, "Yes but only if you help me with something."

"Depends what it is."

She gave me a knowing look, "Walk with me."

I stood up and looked at Lukas who was frowning. I smiled at him, "I'll be back soon." He nodded as Hollie linked her arm through mine. I never thought I would see the day.

"So what's up?" I asked when we reached the bottom of the bleachers.

"I just want to catch up with you and check how you're doing."

I turned to face her, "That's not it so carry on..."

"I saw Isaac today."

My heart leapt at the mention of his name. Is that ever going to stop?

"Oh."

Good one April, well thought out response.

We carried on walking and I realised that we were heading out of the stadium.

"Where are we going?" I asked.

"For a small walk, I need some quiet."

"You, quiet? Ha!"

"I'm so glad that we're friends these days" she replied. I couldn't help but laugh.

We were walking to the spot where Isaac and I had talked last time we were at the game. It stirred up an array of different emotions but mainly hurt as I remembered our painful conversation.

I stopped, "Just spit it out, Hollie.

"Like I said, I saw Isaac today." She watched me, waiting for a response.

I shrugged, trying to look casual. "And?"

"He asked about you."

My attempt to look casual just got a whole lot harder.

"What did he say?" I managed to keep my voice level.

"Just that he's not seen you in a while and asked how you were."

"What did you tell him?"

"I told him that you were good."

I nodded, "So you've brought me out here just to tell me that?"

"He asked if you were dating Lukas."

My heart and mind started racing.

"It's a little strange that he's asking me who you're dating, huh?"

I shrugged, "Maybe he doesn't want any of us getting distracted."

She smiled, "I'm sure that he doesn't."

I couldn't help but ask her the one question that I desperately needed to know, "So what did you say?"

"I told him that he should be asking you that question, not me."

"Is that everything?"

She nodded so I began making my way back to the stadium. I didn't know what to think or feel. It wasn't a big deal, he was just checking how I was doing. But deep down, I knew that it was more than that.

Hollie caught up to me, "He seems to have a real soft spot for you."

I snorted. He sure had a funny way of showing it, I get whiplash from his mood changes.

"Snort all you want but I'm not stupid. I know an interested guy when I see one. Trust me, I spend a lot of time around them."

I rolled my eyes, "Whatever you think, you're wrong."

"Whatever *you* think, *you're* wrong. You're a good person April, you're allowed to be happy. It's not a crime."

But having a relationship with my tutor *is* a crime as it breaks the university's code of conduct. I refuse to get kicked off the course and I'm pretty sure that he doesn't want to lose his job, even though his behaviour sometimes suggests otherwise.

We walked back into the stadium in silence.

"I'm here if you need to talk" she told me as we climbed the stairs back to our seats.

I nodded before sitting down next to Lukas. He smiled and gave me a light kiss on the lips, "What was all that about?" he asked.

Oh shit, I hadn't thought about what I was going to say.

"Oh...um...it was something to do with the cheerleading outfits."

"Oh right, I was starting to worry that she'd kidnapped you."

I smiled and pretended to watch the rest of the game. I wouldn't even be able to tell you who won.

I was starting to think that me and football games didn't mix.

***

The rest of the week was spent counting down the hours until Katie arrived so when Saturday finally came around, it felt like Christmas. I desperately needed some alone time with my best friend. I missed her so much and she always gave me the best, albeit crazy advice.

I was getting ready to go and meet her at the train station when there was a knock on my front door. I thought that it must have been Lukas so I was completely taken aback to see Katie standing there. All tanned skin and blonde hair, she was gorgeous. I squealed whilst jumping up and down. She joined in before throwing her arms around me.

"I've missed you so much" she said.

"I've missed you too."

She pulled away and I could see the tears in her eyes, "Look at you, your hair looks darker and it's getting so long. And you've lost weight" she said whilst spinning me around, getting a good look at me.

I laughed, "It's the student diet. I can't believe that you're actually here."

"I know, I want you to show me everything!"

"Even the library?"

"Even the library, nerds are hot."

"Since when do you like nerds?" I asked.

"Since about ten minutes ago. It's the university air, it goes straight to your head."

"I didn't know there was a university air..."

"Yep, it smells like students - alcohol, sex, takeaway food and dusty old books."

"Wait, is that what I smell like?"

"No...just dusty old books."

"I was going to let you share my bed but now I'm not so sure."

"Then I'll just have to find somebody else's bed to share. Bonus points if he's hot." She wiggled her eyebrows up and down and I couldn't help but laugh.

"You're unbelievable" I told her whilst shaking my head.

"That's what they all say. So where are you taking me first?"

"I can give you a little tour of the campus, take you to the library so you can perve at some nerds?"

She grinned, "Sounds perfect."

***

"I'm bored already."

I laughed, "Katie, it's been twenty minutes. I've only shown you one building."

"Yeah well it's boring and there are no hot guys here."

"It's Saturday, the hot guys are probably hungover in bed."

"Yes please" she replied.

"You're obsessed, you're even worse than you were before."

"It's because I'm sex starved."

"Still?"

"Yep, it's been a month. I'm practically a born again virgin."

"I'm pretty sure that's not what a born again virgin is..."

"Well you would know, frigid."

"You've been here for less than an hour and you're starting already. I am not frigid!"

"Yes you are, I can prove it to you. Take me to the library and we'll look up frigid in the dictionary, it'll have a picture of you as the definition."

I rolled my eyes, "Please explain to me how I am frigid."

"Hmmm let's see, your drop dead gorgeous tutor wants to sleep with you but you won't let him. There's only one explanation - you're frigid."

"I won't *let him* because I'm seeing where things go with Lukas."

"Bullshit. He wanted you long before you started holding hands with Lukas. Fridgitty fridge."

"Do you know how much trouble we could get into?"

"Nobody would need to know, except me of course."

I shrugged, "Well it's never going to happen."

"Well if you're not going to sleep with him, can I have him? He's not *my* tutor..."

"You're a married woman. You're being bad."

"I am. I'm being very, very bad. In fact, I deserve a detention. I might go and hand myself into him now, where's his office?"

"Shut up and come on."

We arrived at the library five minutes later and her face lit up when she saw a group of 'hot nerds'.

"Now remember that it's a library, not a nightclub so behave" I told her.

"I always behave."

***

Most of the guys that she spoke to seemed scared of her but she found her match in a medical student called Jake. I sat and listened to them flirting for five minutes.

"So you're really learning how to save lives, huh?"

"Yeah, somebody's got to."

Really, Jake?

"I think it's very admirable. Could you teach me CPR?"

I stood up and yanked Katie up with me, "Okay, it's time to go. Somebody's had a little too much *university air*."

Jake scowled at me. "It's true, it goes straight to her head" I told him.

"Can I call you?" he asked Katie.

"No, she's married" I quickly replied.

I watched his eyes dart to her left hand. "No ring?" he asked.

I hadn't even noticed.

Katie shrugged, "I'm married, not dead."

He grinned, "So can I call you?"

"No you can't." I dragged her away and didn't let go until we

133

were outside.

"What was all that about?" I asked her.

"Calm down, it's just harmless flirting."

"Giving a guy your number is not just harmless flirting."

"I didn't give him my number."

"Only because I stopped you. Where's your wedding ring?"

"At home."

"Why?"

"Jeez, it's not a crime. I didn't feel like wearing it so I didn't."

"I think you need to ask yourself why you didn't feel like wearing it."

"I already know why."

I waved my hands, indicating for her to carry on.

"Because I want to have fun this weekend. I want to be Katie the nineteen year old, not Katie the wife. I want to talk to people about something other than married life, it's as if there's nothing else to talk about."

"Is that the only reason?"

"Yes."

"So you're happy being married to Ian?"

"Yes, we have our good days and bad days but who doesn't?"

I nodded, "Promise that you'll talk to me if you're unhappy?"

She held my hand, "I promise, now carry on with the tour."

Chapter Seventeen

"A piano bar? Wow, he really does want to impress me."

I laughed, "Don't flatter yourself, apparently it was Dan's idea."

"So then Dan wants to impress me."

"He wants to impress some girl that works there."

"That should be fun to watch. There's nothing better than watching a dick get turned down...literally."

I giggled, "Really? Nothing better? I can think of lots of things..."

She muttered something under her breath.

"What did you say?" I asked.

"Nothing."

I shrugged.

"I said that you would rather go Isaac watching."

I rolled my eyes, why did she always have to bring him into it?

"You make it sound like a hobby. But no, I would rather go *Lukas watching,* you know, the guy who you're about to meet. Speaking of which, I need to lay down some ground rules."

"I think you're forgetting who's the mum here."

"Mums need ground rules too, just look at my mum."

She nodded, "Good point."

My mum was an alcoholic. She liked to tell people that she was a *recovering* alcoholic but the only thing she was recovering from was a hangover caused by the night before.

"Rule number one - be nice."

"I'm always nice" she replied. I raised an eyebrow.

"Rule number two - go easy on the alcohol."

She coughed to disguise her laughter.

"Rule number three - do *not* mention Isaac."

"But what if my life depends on it? Or what if his name is the answer to a million pound question?"

I sighed, "This is a waste of time isn't it?"

"Rules are made to be broken baby girl but don't worry, I'll behave."

"Just please don't scare him off."

"Can we try our outfits on now?"

"Only if you can recite the rules back to me."

She rolled her eyes, "Be nice, don't get drunk and last but not least, make sure I talk about Isaac non-stop." My eyes widened. "Christ I'm joking, April. Don't mention Isaac, I get it. Now let's go and try some dresses on."

***

Almost two hours later, we were dressed and waiting for the taxi to arrive. I was wearing a long, white, Grecian style dress whilst Katie opted for a short black number.

"Look at us in black and white, good versus evil, the angel and the devil."

"You've got that one right" I told her.

Lukas had offered to share a taxi with us but I insisted on meeting him there. The less alone time with Katie the better. It wasn't that I didn't want her to meet him, I was just nervous about it. She is very full on whereas Lukas is pretty much the opposite.

Katie whistled when we arrived at the piano bar, "Very swanky."

I was excited to try somewhere new for a change. It was a modern building with an all glass exterior.

"I hope the drinks aren't stupidly overpriced" she said as we walked in.

"I hope they are, it might stop you from getting too drunk."

"You know it would take more than that to stop me. I would just have to find a handsome man to buy them for me." She pointed at a man standing at the bar, "Someone like him."

I grinned, "Why don't we go and say hello?"

She placed her hand against my forehead, "What's wrong with you? Are you unwell?"

I walked straight up to the man at the bar and kissed him on the cheek. He turned around looking shocked but then relaxed when he realised it was me.

"Katie, this is Lukas. Lukas, I'd like you to meet Katie."

She laughed whilst eyeing him up and down, "I approve."

"Thanks, not that I would listen to you anyway."

"No, you never do." She gave me a knowing look and I shot her one right back.

She pulled Lukas in for a hug, "Nice to meet you, Lukey boy."

I shook my head but he seemed to find it amusing.

"Nice to meet you too. What would you ladies like to drink?"

"A boy after my own heart, vodka and coke please" replied Katie.

"Red wine please" I added.

"Why don't you go and sit down with the others?" He pointed to a nearby table. "I'll bring them over."

Before I could say anything, Katie linked my arm and pulled me away. "Thanks Lukey boy."

"Stop calling him that" I whispered.

"That wasn't one of the rules" she replied before sticking her tongue out.

This was going to be a long night.

As we approached the others, Dan's eyes lit up at the sight of Katie.

"Don't bother, she's married" I told him bluntly.

"I'm Katie" she said, extending her hand out to him. He took it and kissed it.

Gross.

"Nice to meet you Katie, I'm Dan."

She laughed, realising who he was, "Nice to meet you too."

Before we sat down, I caught her wiping her hand on the back of her dress. We sat as far away from Dan as possible but it didn't stop him from ogling her all night.

***

A couple of hours later and I had stopped worrying about Katie. I liked to think that it was because she was on her best behaviour but it probably had more to do with the alcohol that she kept acquiring for us.

She seemed to genuinely like Lukas which made me happy. Even though we teased each other, I valued her opinion above anybody else's.

When she asked me to go to the ladies room with her, I was eager to ask what she thought about him.

"So?" I asked as soon as we got inside. She began applying lipstick in the mirror.

"I like him" she said. I beamed as I got my own lipstick out of my bag.

"He's very sweet, I just wonder if you'll get bored" she added.

My face fell, "Why would I get bored?"

138

"Because he's too nice and I know what you're like."

"Oh thanks, what's that supposed to mean?"

"You need excitement, someone to keep you on your toes."

"I'm glad you're such an expert on my life. Can you hang on a minute whilst I get a pen and paper to make notes?"

She laughed. "I can wait. But seriously, I don't feel the spark between you two. There's no sexual tension, it's all cuddles and hand holding."

"Why are you saying that like it's a bad thing?"

"Because you're both young and hot. You should want to rip each other's clothes off, not just hold hands."

"We're in a bar...a classy bar."

She shrugged, "So what? You could go in the toilets. Look, my point is, you're not even considering it."

"I'm so sorry that I'm not considering having sex with him in a toilet cubicle."

"Honey, when you meet the right one, you won't even make it to the toilet cubicle."

I rolled my eyes, "Whatever, I need another drink." I walked out of the ladies room feeling a little pissed off. Did she have a valid point? I was attracted to him and we came close to having sex the night of the poker game but I didn't feel the urge to rip his clothes off. I definitely didn't feel the urge to have sex with him in the toilets.

"Food for thought?" she asked me.

I shrugged and carried on walking towards the bar. As we approached, we saw Dan talking to a stunning blonde woman behind the bar.

"She's definitely out of his league" Katie whispered to me. I nodded in agreement.

"How long have you been a bartender?" We heard him ask.

139

"I'm the manager here" she replied.

I didn't think it was possible but he looked even more smitten by her.

"What time do you get off work?"

"Two. My boyfriend's taking me home."

"He's a very lucky guy."

"I'm the lucky one, he's very protective over me."

Dan held his hands up, "Message loud and clear but if you change your mind, you know where I am."

I tried my best not to laugh but a small giggle escaped my lips.

"Crash and burn" Katie muttered under her breath.

He scowled at us on his way back to the table. We ordered our drinks and then joined the rest of the group.

"I got her number, we're meeting up next week" Dan was telling them.

Katie burst out laughing, "Is her overprotective boyfriend going too?"

He frowned but then winked at her, "He can come if he wants. Some dudes enjoy watching their chick get nailed by somebody else."

I think Dan liked the fact that Katie gave as good as she got. Of course, it didn't hurt that she was drop dead gorgeous too. Thank god that she was married. Before Ian, Katie seemed to be attracted to douche bags. Dan would have fit the bill perfectly.

She rolled her eyes, "That only happens in porn."

"Oh my god, you watch porn?" asked Dan.

Just as I was trying to think of a different topic of conversation, I remembered that I had left my lipstick in the ladies room.

I nudged Katie, "I've left my lipstick in the ladies, I'm going to get it."

She nodded and carried on talking to Dan.

I smiled at Lukas as I stood up, "I'll be back in a minute."

"Everything okay?" he asked.

"Fine."

I felt a little wobbly from the alcohol so I walked slowly, holding both of my hands out to steady myself. Just as I was about to enter the ladies room, a strong hand grabbed me around the waist whilst another clamped across my mouth. I panicked and kicked out as hard as I could but the alcohol slowed me down. I tried screaming but his hand was pressed too tightly against my mouth.

We entered some kind of stock room and I kicked out again. This time I was successful as my foot collided with a body part. My attacker let out a moan before spinning me around so that I was facing them. I was about to headbutt them when my eyes nearly popped out of my head.

Isaac was staring back at me whilst shushing me like a baby. It took my body a few seconds to catch up with my brain and stop fighting him. He had completely scared the shit out of me. I thought I was being attacked by some lunatic. What was wrong with a simple hello or another one of his charming phone calls?

"Please don't scream" he said before slowly taking his hand away from my mouth.

"What the fuck are you doing?" I asked him.

My emotions were already running high from the alcohol and my conversation with Katie so he had chosen the completely wrong time to kidnap me. I felt like kissing him and hitting him at the same time. I wanted to run away but stay in his arms forever. As per usual, Isaac Sharpe made me feel completely crazy. Sending for the men in white coats crazy.

"Watch your language" he replied.

I stared at him. Was he for real? I was pretty sure that he didn't go to all of this trouble just to lecture me about my use of language.

"Don't tell me to watch my fucking language. What the fuck just happened?"

He looked angry.

Join the club.

"Are you trying to kill me?" he asked, his piercing blue eyes more intense than ever.

"WHAT? You're the one who has just given me a goddamn heart attack!" I shouted.

He looked me up and down, "It's bad enough that I can't have you but then you turn up here looking like that."

"Looking like *what*?" I asked, offended by his comment.

He shook his head, "You really don't have a clue, do you?"

"No! I don't have a clue what's happening, I don't have a clue why we're in a stock room and I don't have a fucking clue why you're holding me like I'm about to run away."

"Well you've ran away from me before. Ran away from us." I could feel the hurt in his voice and it cut me deep.

I realised that his arm was still wrapped around my waist, pulling my body into his. I was suddenly very aware of how my breasts were pressed up against his warm, hard chest. My nipples grew hard, tingling with lust. I had a love/hate relationship with the way that he made me feel. I tried to wriggle free but it only made him tighten his grip.

"Why are you here?" he asked.

"I forgot how charming you were."

"Answer the question, April."

"I'm here with my friends, what's the big fucking deal?"

"I've told you to watch your language."

"Watch your fucking language" I spat in reply.

Good one.

He raised an eyebrow, looking amused.

I wriggled again but it was only a half-hearted attempt, "Let me go, Isaac."

"Keep saying my name like that and you won't be going anywhere tonight except from home with me."

I gasped when I felt him grow hard. I was so worked up that it was nearly enough to undo me right there on the spot. My breathing turned heavy as my head swam with desire. I wanted to touch him, to feel him against my bare skin.

I could feel the sexual tension dripping off us and just like Katie had said, I found myself wanting to rip all of his clothes off. I wanted him to take me, dominate me, own me. I didn't care that we were in a damn stock room, we could have been anywhere for all I cared. The whole world fell away at our feet and all that mattered was us.

His eyes were wild and hungry as he leant in and brushed his lips across my neck. He took a deep breath, inhaling my scent before flicking his tongue up and down. He began tracing different shapes with the tip of his tongue and I moaned in delight, wishing that it was teasing a different part of my body.

"Do you like that, April? Do you like how my tongue feels against your skin?" His voice was so throaty and husky, I swear I felt it vibrate through my entire body.

When his tongue found my skin once more, my hips bucked, pressing his erection right in-between my thighs where I craved him the most. I moved up and down, rubbing him against me. I started off slow but increased the pace when he began moving with me. I could feel the pressure started to build and with each flick of his tongue, I got closer and closer to finding my release.

My body craved him. My heart craved him. Even my head now craved him.

I closed my eyes and surrendered to the wave of pleasure that crashed over me. A moan escaped my lips just as I heard my name being called from outside.

Oh no. It was Lukas.

My body was still shuddering in response to the orgasm and I bit Isaac's shoulder to stop from crying out. He growled, which only helped to prolong my pleasure.

When my body finally relaxed, he took my face in his hands and gently stroked my cheek with his thumb. He wasn't worried or panicked, just completely calm. His eyes were no longer dark and intense but full of passion and adoration which made the butterflies in my stomach go crazy.

Typical, he even made the damn butterflies go crazy.

Then without saying a word, he dropped his hands to his side and released me from him. I slowly turned away and took a couple of deep breaths, trying to compose myself before reaching for the door handle.

When I left the stock room, it was like stepping into a whole new world - reality. The guilt hit me like a ton of bricks. I just had the best orgasm of my life whilst Lukas was standing right outside. Lord knows what it would feel like if Isaac was ever actually inside me. I shook my head, trying to erase the thought from my mind.

This time, I actually went into the ladies room and picked up my lipstick off the vanity before splashing my face with cold water. I was paranoid that I smelt like him so began to wash my hands and arms. But for some fucked up reason, I couldn't bring myself to wash my neck where he had licked me. It was pulsating with pleasure and I could still feel his lips on my skin. I was shaking from the adrenaline.

Why was he even here tonight? Was it just a coincidence that we were both at the same club? Was I going to have to see him again when I walked out?

I wondered how long I had been gone for, obviously long enough to make Lukas come looking for me. How could I have done this to him? Not only did I have genuine feelings for him but he was one of my best friends too. He didn't deserve to be treated this way.

I felt like a crazy woman. It had been one of the best

144

experiences of my life but now I felt ashamed. I tried to convince myself that it wasn't actually that bad, I hadn't had sex with him or even kissed him for that matter. No, the scary thing was how much I wanted to do those things.

I jumped when the door opened and Katie walked in.

"There you are. Where have you been? Lukas is getting worried."

"I told you, I left my lipstick."

"Why has it taken you ten minutes to get it? Lukas said he knocked on the door and shouted but you didn't answer."

"I didn't hear him. I don't feel good."

I hated lying to her but I couldn't bring myself to tell her the truth. For one, it would become more real if I talked about it out loud and for two, she would make me end things with Lukas. I knew it was selfish of me but I didn't want to lose him. I wanted to see if I could feel as passionate about him as I did about Isaac. I wanted to see if we had a future together, one where we didn't have to sneak around in stock rooms.

"Are you okay?" she asked, wrapping both of her arms around me.

I felt like crying but managed to hold it together, "Yeah I just feel sick, do you mind if we go home?"

"That's fine with me baby girl, Dan's starting to annoy me anyway."

"Starting to?"

As we walked back to the table, I looked around for Isaac but couldn't see him anywhere.

Lukas rushed up to me and I could barely look him in the eye. "Are you okay?" he asked.

"I'm fine but I don't feel good. Too much alcohol again."

He took hold of my hand and I felt awful. "I came looking for you."

"I know" I said before panicking, "Katie told me."

"You started to worry me." He kissed me on the head and I couldn't take anymore.

"I'm sorry. We're going home now."

"Do you want me to come with you?"

"No, you stay. I'll talk to you tomorrow."

"Are you sure you're okay?" I could see the concern in his eyes.

I nodded. We said bye to the rest of the group before making our way out of the club and into a taxi.

When we got home, we got changed into our pyjamas before both climbing into my double bed. She fell asleep straight away but I knew that I wouldn't be so lucky.

I hardly slept but when I did, I dreamt about Isaac and of course, the stock room.

Chapter Eighteen

When Katie finally got out of bed the next morning, she was surprisingly upbeat. I was already lounging on the sofa watching TV.

"No hangover then?" I asked.

"A small one but I don't care. I slept for eight hours straight, eight hours! That's a miracle when you've got a baby. I feel so refreshed."

I laughed, "At least someone does."

"Do you still feel bad?"

Yes, about a lot of things.

I shrugged, "I'm more upset that you're leaving me in a few hours."

She sighed, "I know, it's been awesome seeing you. I miss you so much."

"I miss you too."

"Stop it now, you're going to make me cry. So what are we going to do for the next couple of hours?" she asked.

"There's not much to do on a Sunday morning. We could go for some breakfast?"

"Sounds like a plan."

We walked to the campus coffee shop and ordered a cappuccino and a blueberry muffin each. Katie chose a table by the window which was nice as the window seats were usually always taken in the week. I sat facing outside, with my back to the rest of the shop. I liked sitting here, I could watch the leaves blowing in the wind and it made sitting inside with a hot drink seem cosy. A few people walked past and glanced inside but after a while, I didn't even notice them. I took a sip of my cappuccino and began telling her all about my course. After about ten minutes, I could see her looking over my shoulder. I thought she was getting bored of listening to me talk about coursework so I changed the topic.

"So what else am I missing back home?"

"Absolutely nothing, it looks like you've got everything you need right here."

"What do you mean by that?" I asked.

"Don't turn around but there's an insanely hot guy standing at the counter."

I resisted the urge to turn around.

"He's completely edible. Am I drooling?"

I laughed, "Not yet but I need to look."

"Okay but play it cool."

I didn't know how I could possibly make turning around look cool so I glanced over my right shoulder which was away from the counter and then over my left, towards the counter.

Seriously, was I cursed or something? Had I broken a mirror or walked under some ladders without remembering? Maybe I had been really bad in my past life.

Isaac was leaning against the counter wearing a plain white t-shirt that clung to his six pack and a pair of low slung sweatpants. I wanted to take them off and lick him all over his body the way that he had licked me last night, starting with his abs.

This was bad.

I groaned and turned back to Katie, "We need to leave right now."

"With him? Hell yeah. Not sure if Blondie's going to be happy about it though, she's got her hands all over him."

Blondie? I didn't see any Blondie.

I couldn't help myself, I looked over my shoulder again and thought that I was going to throw up. It was the gorgeous blonde woman from the piano bar. The one who mentioned that she had a boyfriend and by the way she was whispering in his ear, it didn't take a genius to work out that it was Isaac. Is that why he was at the piano bar last night? It was all starting to add up. Except the part where he dragged me into the stock room and rubbed against me until I had a mind blowing orgasm.

Just when I thought things couldn't get any worse, he looked in our direction.

I turned back around. "We need to go, please. I'll explain once we're outside."

She looked at me with narrowed eyes then shrugged, "You're crazy. I'm taking this with me though." She picked up her mug of coffee.

"Just leave the coffee, I'll buy you another one later."

She groaned, "But I really want it."

"Katie, please."

She sighed, "I'm only doing this because I love you."

"Thank you." I expected her to put the mug down but instead I watched as she downed it in less than five seconds.

"I've just burnt my throat for you. Let's roll."

There was no way of avoiding him. There was only one way in and one way out.

"Keep talking to me" I told Katie as we stood up and made our way over to the exit.

"Why?"

"Just keep talking. Say something funny, tell me a joke."

"Why did the girl down a scorching cup of coffee?"

"I don't know, why did the girl down a scorching cup of coffee?" I asked, putting on a fake smile.

"Because her best friend has gone bananas."

I laughed like it was the funniest joke on earth. She narrowed her eyes at me, "It wasn't that funny, I can't wait to hear what's going on when we get outside."

I kept my eyes fixed on Katie until she checked Isaac out as we passed the counter. I looked down and muttered "keep walking" under my breath, refusing to look anywhere other than my feet.

Relief flooded through me when we stepped outside but I didn't stop walking until there was a safe distance between us and the coffee shop. I was half expecting him to run out after me. I sat down on a nearby bench and took a few deep breaths, willing my heart beat to return to its normal rhythm. I felt like crying and screaming at the same time. I also felt like going and beating the shit out of him for making me feel this way. Images of last night flashed through my mind followed by the image of Blondie laughing and whispering in his ear. I was starting to feel really angry. Why did he pull me into the stock room last night when he has a girlfriend?

Katie sat down next to me and looked at me expectantly, "Well?"

"The guy you were drooling over back there...it was Isaac."

Her eyes nearly popped out of her head, "Tutor Isaac? *Isaac Isaac?*"

I nodded.

"No fucking way!" she shouted, causing a passer-by to look over at us.

"Yes fucking way."

"No. Fucking. Way."

I shrugged, "Okay, don't believe me."

"I don't believe you. Do you want to know why? Because no sane person would turn *that* down." She began shaking her head, "I was right, you *are* crazy."

"Yes but only because he makes me crazy! I hear a song, I think about Isaac. I go to class, I think about Isaac. I go to sleep and I fucking dream about Isaac. I give up, I can't do it anymore. You know what's even crazier? To even consider getting kicked out of my first choice university for him. You know how hard I've worked to get a place here, not to mention the grant that I earned. I'm not risking it. I'd

150

be left with nothing but shattered dreams and an alcoholic mother."

Katie looked completely taken aback. "So that's all it took, huh? All this time, you've tried to deny your true feelings for him then you see him with another woman and the truth comes flooding out."

I shrugged.

"Wow, I should have paid somebody to grope him in front of you a long time ago. Actually, I wouldn't even have to pay them, they would probably do it for free."

"I'm being serious, Katie."

"I know you are, that's my point. You have serious feelings for Isaac."

"Had, not have."

"If it was past tense then you wouldn't be so worked up about it now. You know, just because they were together doesn't mean that they're dating. She's probably just one of his groupies, maybe she carries his books around and leaves an apple on his desk."

"Katie, did you even see who it was? She's the manager of the piano bar."

"And?"

"And you heard what she said to Dan last night. She's got a boyfriend, Isaac is obviously her boyfriend."

She shook her head, "I don't believe it."

"What's not to believe? You even said it yourself, she had her hands all over him."

"I don't believe that Isaac would date someone like her. She's probably cheating on her boyfriend *with* Isaac."

I rolled my eyes, "Oh that makes it so much better."

"I'm just saying that you shouldn't jump to conclusions."

"Stop defending him. Why are you Team Isaac all of a sudden?"

"Are you joking? I've got eyes, that's a good enough reason to be Team Isaac."

"Yeah well I've got eyes too and it's clear that he's moved on so he should leave me alone."

And stop dragging me into stock rooms.

"April..."

"No, I'm done. No more Isaac. I can't do it anymore. There's a reason that he's my tutor, it's not meant to be."

"Oh don't give me all that fate bullshit."

"Well it's true."

"No it's not true. I could turn around and say that there was a reason why you were late on your first day. If you weren't late then you wouldn't have ran into him. There's a reason you met him, you were meant to meet him. So don't start with all of that. Life is what you make of it."

"You've got to admit that it's strange that we were in the same coffee shop at the same time."

"Oh yeah, it's really strange that two people who like coffee and presumably live near each other went to the same coffee shop" she said, sarcastically.

I ignored her, "I needed to see him with another woman to make me realise that I have to move on." I pointed to the coffee shop, "*That* was my closure."

She groaned.

"I'm done. No more Isaac, you're not even allowed to mention his name anymore."

"What about the t-shirts I've ordered?"

"What t-shirts?"

"My Team Isaac ones."

"Can you be serious for just one minute?"

She rolled her eyes and shook her head, "Okay, I get it. No more Isaac, good luck with that."

"What are you trying to say? Spit it out."

"You've just been on the verge of having a mental break down because you saw him with another woman and now you expect me to believe that you're *done*?" Her use of air speech marks on the word 'done' really pissed me off.

"Yes, I do expect you to believe me because you're my best friend. You're supposed to support me no matter what, not argue with me."

"I'm just trying to be honest with you but you don't like it."

"You're not being honest, you're being a bitch."

"If telling you the truth is being a bitch then yes, I'm a bitch."

"Please just support me and stop with the whole Isaac thing. I know that you're hoping that one day we will get married and live happily ever after but this isn't some cheesy love story, this is my life."

She looked genuinely upset. "Why are *you* upset?" I asked.

"Because I am. I don't want you to give up, you don't see what I see. You don't see how crazy you are about each other or the way that he looked at you just then."

"I see it alright, I don't see anything else. I play out the first time we met over and over again in my head. It's stuck on repeat. I see it. I feel it. But that's the problem. You even said it yourself, I nearly had a mental breakdown. That's not good for me, *he's* not good for me. He's making me crazy."

She scooted closer and put her arm around me, "I just want you to get what you deserve."

"Yes, I deserve a man who makes me feel safe like Lukas."

"No. You deserve a man who makes you feel *butterflies*. Love isn't safe. Love is crazy and scary and unpredictable. You can't control it and you sure as hell can't fight it. It's one of life's greatest risks...but it's also one of life's greatest gifts."

"So you're trying to tell me that crazy and scary is good?"

"Yes. Crazy, good. Boring, bad."

I shook my head, "Whatever you say, cave girl."

We stayed silent for a short while, watching the trees sway in the wind.

"I love you, A. I will support you no matter what."

"I love you too."

After a moment, she began to shake her head again. "You didn't tell me how hot he is."

"I'm pretty sure I did."

"You said that he was hot. You didn't tell me that he was *smoking* hot, I bet you could cook food on his abs."

I laughed at the mental image that she had just created for me.

"I would have visited a lot sooner if I had known" she said, grinning.

"That's why I didn't tell you."

"Well you've got a lot of self-restraint, I'll give you that. I'd be all over him like a rash."

"You seriously need to put your wedding ring back on."

"You seriously need to have babies with him, they would be so gorgeous."

"What did I say about not talking about him?

She looked at me all innocent, "I thought you just meant that I wasn't allowed to say his name."

I shook my head, "It's a good job that I love you."

***

We both cried when it was time to say goodbye. Even though

we spoke on the phone nearly every day, it wasn't the same. She took my hands in hers, "Life is one big risk, you just need to recognise which risks are worth taking." I nodded and hugged her tightly.

I waited until her train pulled out of the station before heading back home. She had done a good job of distracting me since our conversation about Isaac but now it was just me and my overactive imagination. In the time it took me to walk home, I had already imagined Isaac and Blondie in every sexual position that I could think of. How could Katie ever think that crazy was a good thing?

After torturing myself, I was left feeling frustrated and more determined than ever to prove that I didn't need Isaac. I had a good thing going with Lukas and it was time to take our relationship to the next level. I saw a future with Lukas, one which was loving and carefree. I wanted to make up for last night and I knew what I was going to do.

Chapter Nineteen

I knocked on his door, hoping that he was home alone. When he answered, he looked happy and I was relieved to see his smiling face. Whatever Katie might think, it was important to feel safe in a relationship. All girls wanted security.

He was wearing shorts and nothing else. He looked sweaty, like he had just been working out. It was the first time that I was seeing him without a shirt on and I mentally kicked myself for not insisting on it sooner. I somehow managed to pull my eyes away from his abs and up to meet his gaze.

"Are you okay?" he asked.

I nodded, "Better now. Are you alone?"

"Yeah, Dan won't be back until late."

"Can I come in?"

"Of course."

As soon as he closed the door, I couldn't wait any longer. I pushed him up against the door and kissed him with everything that I had. I wanted Lukas. I wanted his abs pressed up against my bare skin. I wanted to feel the sparks that I had felt last night with Isaac. I remembered the way that he had licked my neck as I pressed my body up against Lukas. My hands began to explore his body. I loved how the softness of his skin contrasted with the hard lines of his abs. I could feel how fast his heart was beating, in a race against mine.

"Are you sure?" he asked with caution in his eyes.

"I'm sure" I kissed him again but could feel that his body was still tense.

I looked up at him, "Lukas, I want this." I wanted to prove that I could have a connection with somebody else. That somebody else could make my body react in the same way that it did for Isaac. I had genuine feelings for Lukas so it wasn't like I was doing anything wrong.

"Do you want to talk about it first?"

Ever the gentleman.

156

"No, I want you to kiss me."

He took my hand and led me into his bedroom. I sat down on the edge of his bed and I thought I saw a flash of indecision in his eyes but it was quickly replaced with desire as he pulled down his shorts. I unfastened the buttons on my jeans before he pulled them off and climbed on top of me. He pressed his hard body against mine and my hips bucked in response.

"I just want you to know that I wouldn't be doing this unless I was absolutely sure that I was in love with you."

Wow.

I was caught off guard by his confession but it also reassured me that we were doing the right thing. This kind, intelligent man loved me and I desperately wanted to love him back.

He stared into my eyes whilst slowly removing each article of clothing. I pulled his boxer shorts down and gasped when I felt his erection pressing against my thigh. He kissed me as he leant over and retrieved something from the bedside table. I watched him tear open the foil packet before closing my eyes, preparing myself for what was about to happen next.

He slowly entered me and I instantly forgot about everything else apart from him. He kept his eyes on mine the whole time and I knew how much it meant to him. This was more than just sex.

I threw my head back and moved my body in time with his. We began to pick up the pace and I adjusted my body so that he could thrust deeper inside me.

"April..."

"Don't stop" I ordered as I clenched around him, desperately searching for my own source of pleasure.

He carried on thrusting into me before I felt his body tense up and he called out my name. He pressed his forehead against mine and I allowed my body to relax.

He held me in his arms for a long time afterwards whilst I tried to block out the emotions that were threatening to drown me.

Happiness, sadness, frustration and guilt were currently battling against each other.

"I'll give you a minute to get dressed" he said as he sat up and pulled his shorts back on before walking out of the room.

I closed my eyes and just laid there for a few moments before getting dressed.

He smiled as I walked into the living room, "You okay?"

I nodded.

"Do you want to stay for dinner?" he asked.

"I would but I'm really tired, I didn't sleep much last night." His smile faded. "Can we reschedule?" I asked.

"Yeah, that's fine. Come here."

He wrapped his arms around me and held me tight, "Do you want to talk about anything?"

"No, do you?"

He shook his head, "As long as you're okay. You surprised me turning up like that."

"I'm sorry."

"Don't be." He kissed me on the forehead, "Do you want me to walk you home?"

"No, it's fine. I'll see you tomorrow."

I walked home as fast as I could and the moment I got inside, I broke down. Why was I feeling so emotional? I hadn't expected to feel this way. I thought my mind would be clearer. I thought that I would prove to myself that Lukas could make me happy in more ways than one.

I guess this is what happens when your head and your heart pull you in completely opposite directions.

***

By the time Monday morning rolled around, I was emotionally and physically drained. After another sleepless night, I was relying on coffee to keep me awake. So it didn't help that I spilt it everywhere when I was trying to get my phone out of my pocket. I snapped at the guy from the library who had rung to tell me that they were experiencing 'technical difficulties' with my email account.

"Is it really important enough to ring me? Are you purposely trying to make me feel worse than I already do?"

"Um...no. You might not be able to use your account for a while so we have to warn you."

After being a total bitch and hanging up on him, I made another cup of coffee which tasted like crap but I refused to step foot in the campus coffee shop. I managed not to spill it this time and drank it before heading to class.

I sat down in my first lecture and saved a seat for Lukas but he never arrived. After class, I checked my phone and had a text message from him -

"Hey. How are you? I don't feel good, think I might have caught a stomach bug. Hopefully see you tomorrow x"

It was probably just as well seeing as though I was in a horrible mood. I text back telling him to feel better and then plodded through the rest of my day alone.

When Lukas didn't show up for classes on Tuesday or Wednesday, I started to worry that it might have something to do with Sunday night. I rang him on Wednesday lunch time and he didn't sound himself, he sounded even more tired than I was. He said that he was starting to feel better though and asked if he could come and see me tonight. I told him to stay in bed and that I would go to his place instead but he insisted on coming to mine. He mentioned something about needing time away from Dan.

I rang Katie whilst I was waiting for Lukas to arrive. When she picked up, there was crying in the background. I moved the phone away from my ear, "Hey Kitty."

"He's punishing me for being away from him at the weekend."

"Who, Ian?" I joked.

"Jamie, he's been crying all day."

"Something happened with Lukas" I blurted out. I needed to tell her.

"Oh no, what could have possibly happened since Sunday? Your life is like a soap opera."

"We had sex."

I heard her say something to Ian before the crying got quieter. She must have gone into another room. After a long pause she spoke, "Are you sure that was the right thing to do?"

"What do you mean?"

"Well your emotions were running high when I left. Did you do it for the right reasons?"

"Of course I did it for the right reasons." I doubted myself as soon as I said it.

"I don't know, maybe you should have waited."

"For how long? You were calling me frigid at weekend and now you're making out like I rushed into it, make your mind up."

"I think you should have waited until *your* mind was made up."

"My mind was made up, or do you not remember the conversation that we had outside the coffee shop?"

She sighed, "Of course I remember. I just think you should have waited until you were completely over you-know-who."

"Who, Voldemort?"

"April, you know who I mean."

"I am over him."

"I said *completely* over him."

Fuck.

"How do you feel about what happened? Are you happy?"

"I don't know, I'm seeing him again tonight. I want to be happy but I think my brain is trying to sabotage my relationship with him."

"Just take things slow, see what happens. I'm happy if you're happy and you know I'm here for you."

"I know, thank you."

"Ring me if you need me."

"Will do."

***

When Lukas arrived, he pulled me into a big bear hug which immediately made me feel better.

"How are you feeling?" I asked when he pulled away.

"Like crap."

"Oh. You didn't have to come over, you should have stayed in bed."

His eyes looked glassy, almost like he was about to cry, "Hey, are you okay?"

He shook his head, "Can we sit down?"

"Of course." My heartbeat picked up speed as I led him over to the sofa. He sat down and stared at me as though he was trying to memorise my face. The pain in his eyes was so obvious that it made my heart ache. "Lukas, what's wrong?"

"Please don't hate me."

"I could never hate you."

He shook his head and I got a sick feeling in the pit of my stomach.

"I need to tell you something but I'm scared that you'll never speak to me again. Please hear me out."

161

"You're scaring me now, just tell me." I took a deep breath and held it, bracing myself for whatever he was about to say.

"There's no easy way to say this, I should have told you from day one. I was engaged."

I slowly let my breath out, "When?"

"It's complicated."

"How is it complicated? Was it last year? This year?"

"This year."

I felt more confused than anything else, "Okay...so when did it end?"

"Yesterday."

I just stared at him, my mind unable to process what he was saying. I waited for him to tell me that it was all a big joke but when a tear fell down his cheek, I knew that he was telling the truth. I shook my head, completely speechless.

"April, I'm sorry. I love you."

He tried to move closer to me but I backed away, "Don't say that. Don't tell me that you love me when you're engaged to another woman."

"I'm not, I ended it."

"Is that supposed to make me feel better?" I was already an emotional wreck and this felt like the nail in the coffin. I was angry but couldn't stop the tears from flowing, "So all this time, you've been engaged?"

"Technically..."

"What sort of bullshit answer is technically? You let us sleep together. How could you? What sort of person does that? I thought we were friends."

"We are."

I shook my head, "Not anymore. I can't believe you betrayed

me like that."

"I was scared that I would lose you."

I threw my hands up, "But you've lost me now anyway."

"April, please..."

"Get out of my house."

He stood up, "I was going to tell you, I was. But then I started falling in love with you and I was afraid that you wouldn't want to be with me if you knew."

"You're damn right I wouldn't, you belonged to someone else!"

"No, I've always belonged to you."

"Well I don't belong to you" I spat out. I could see how deep my words cut him.

"Please just leave."

"Let me tell you the full story."

"I don't want to hear the full story, I've heard enough. I thought you were a good person, I was wrong."

I walked to the door and he followed, "Please send my sincerest apologies to your fiancée." He took hold of my hand but I yanked it away, "Don't." I couldn't bear to look him in the eye.

His voice cracked, "I never wanted to hurt you."

The most depressing thing was that I actually believed him.

I locked the door behind him and then dropped to the floor and cried. I curled up into a ball and let it all out. I was in total shock. Lukas was the last person that I thought would ever do something like this. I never thought that he would be capable of cheating on a woman, let alone his fiancée. He was so caring and loyal. It just goes to show how wrong I was. My judgement was completely off the mark. If I couldn't trust Lukas then who could I trust? I began to doubt all of the choices that I had made including the one to walk away from Isaac.

I kept expecting to wake up from a bad dream but it never happened. I cried for a long time. Even though I had questioned my relationship with Lukas, I did have strong feelings for him and could see him in my future. He was a big part of my life and now I felt like I had lost my best friend. How could I not tell that he was hiding something? Was it my fault for spending so much time thinking about Isaac? Would it have been obvious to someone with a clear head? I felt sick when I thought about us sleeping together. Katie was right, I should have thought about it more. I had rushed into it and this was my punishment. I had been his mistress. Now here I was, feeling guilty for not asking him if he was single before we had sex. I thought it was pretty safe of me to presume that he didn't have a fiancée. I not only felt sorry for myself but for her, whoever she was. Had she already bought her wedding dress? I had broken an engagement up and had to live with that for the rest of my life.

I also questioned whether I was being a hypocrite. After what had happened in the stock room with Isaac, did I really have a leg to stand on? Was I any better? Although I still felt guilty about it, I came to the conclusion that it was completely different. I didn't go out that night with the intentions of it happening. I wasn't in a relationship with Isaac and I definitely wasn't engaged to him. So yes, it was different or at least, that's what I told myself.

I cried a lot that night. I also drank a lot. I liked it when I got to the point where I couldn't think straight, it was an escape from reality. The problems were still there, but they didn't feel half as bad. I eventually drank myself to sleep.

Chapter Twenty

I spent the next two days sleeping. When I wasn't sleeping, I was crying. My eyes were red and puffy and I had no appetite whatsoever, although my stomach kept rumbling in protest. I didn't even have the motivation to brush my hair so I certainly wasn't going to any of my classes. I hadn't spoken to anyone since Lukas had left and I wanted to keep it that way. I had switched my mobile off on Wednesday and had no intention of turning it back on again anytime soon. I was embarrassed and didn't want anybody's pity.

I was in a dark place. So much so that on Friday it seemed like a good idea to drink half a bottle of vodka. It seemed like an even better idea to drink half a bottle of vodka whilst watching *'The Notebook'*.

Epic fail.

Half a bottle of vodka and a box of tissues later, I jumped when there was a knock on my front door. I glanced at the clock, it was almost five thirty in the evening. I stayed sat on the sofa and muted the TV. I wasn't going to answer it, I was in my pyjamas and hadn't had a wash or brushed my teeth in two days. Plus, I was drunk. I would struggle to even stand up without falling over.

Whoever it was carried on knocking until I heard my name being called. I immediately recognised his smooth and sexy voice.

Isaac.

I was instantly relieved that it wasn't Lukas but there was still no way that I was going to let Isaac see me in this state. I was also pissed off at him after seeing him and Blondie together at the coffee shop.

He was shouting through the letterbox now, "April, are you in there? Please open the door. I'm worried about you." When I didn't respond he carried on, "I just want to check that you're okay, then I'll leave."

I could hear the genuine concern in his voice. I stood up but my head started spinning. I wobbled and fell back down onto the sofa. I tried again but this time slower, steadying myself using the sofa arm. I managed to stand up and very slowly walk over to the door.

"April, is that you?"

"Yes." My voice came out shaky. I hadn't heard myself talk in almost two days. I leant my back against the wall and slid down it until I was sitting down.

"Are you okay?"

"Yes" I lied.

"Are you unwell?"

I closed my eyes and thought for a moment, debating whether to carry on lying to him. For some reason, I wanted to tell him the truth. The room started spinning even worse so I opened my eyes, "No." Tears began to roll down my cheeks and a sob escaped my lips.

"Are you crying? Let me in."

I didn't want him to see me like this but I desperately craved some attention. I needed him to make me feel better and hear that everything was going to be okay. I slowly got to my feet and unlocked the door.

The look on Isaac's face was a mixture of shock, hurt and anger.

"April, come here." He wrapped his arms around me and held me tightly. I tried to keep my emotions under check but they all came flooding out. I began sobbing into his chest whilst he stroked my hair, trying to soothe me.

"It's okay, don't cry. I'm here. I'm not going anywhere."

We stayed like that for a long while and when I eventually stopped crying, he led me over to the sofa. He was about to sit down next to me when he noticed the empty bottle of vodka and picked it up.

"Have you drunk all of this today?"

"Half a bottle" I replied, feeling embarrassed and a little bit ashamed.

"Have you had anything to eat?"

I shook my head.

"I'll make you something."

"Please, I'm not hungry."

He ignored me and left the room. I flattened my hair down and went to pick up the wet tissues off the floor but my head pounded. I decided it was best to just sit down and leave it. He had seen me in this state so the damage was already done.

He walked back in five minutes later and handed me a bowl of soup, "Chicken soup for the soul" he announced.

I tried to smile but I think it came out as more of a grimace.

"Come on, just eat it slowly. I'll sit here and feed it to you if I have to."

I picked up the spoon and took a small mouthful. It tasted good. Really good. It was only then that I realised how starving I was. I had survived the past two days on yoghurts and whatever chocolate I had in the house. Isaac watched me in silence until I finished it.

"Nice?" he asked.

"Yes, thank you."

He took the bowl off me and set it down on the coffee table. I didn't feel quite as drunk now that I had some food in my stomach.

"April, you should have called me. If I'd have known sooner..."

"I'm not your problem."

He laughed, "You're joking right? You're my *only* problem."

"Well thanks for that."

"April, what's happened? You've missed two days worth of lectures and I know that Lukas has been absent too."

My stomach churned at the mention of his name and I felt like I was going to throw up.

"Has he hurt you?"

"No…well yes…" I watched as his eyes turned angry. "Not physically" I added.

He closed his eyes and took a deep breath, "Tell me what he's done."

I really didn't want to get into it, especially with Isaac. But I knew that he wasn't going to let it drop and I'd rather him hear it from me than Lukas. I just hoped that he didn't go looking for Lukas afterwards. "He's engaged, well he was until he broke it off this week."

His hands clenched into fists as his breathing turned heavy. I had never seen him look so angry, even when he saw Lukas kiss my hand in the seminar weeks ago.

"What a fucking scum bag. I knew he wasn't good enough for you, I can't believe I let this happen." He began shaking his head.

"This had nothing to do with you, you couldn't have stopped it."

His eyes turned fiery and intense, "Trust me, I could have."

We sat in silence for a moment whilst I tried to work out what that even meant.

"I'm the only one who should feel guilty" I whispered.

"Guilty? Why?"

"I've broken an engagement off."

"Did you know that he was engaged?"

"No, of course not."

"Then it's not your fault. He's the guilty one, he's hurt and betrayed two women. I'm so angry, the only reason I'm not out there looking for him right now is because you need me more."

"This isn't your fight."

"Just like the sky isn't blue?"

When I didn't respond, he stood up, "I'm going to run you a bath and then go and buy you some food."

"Isaac, no. You don't have to."

"Yes, I do. Please just let me do this for you."

I nodded then watched as he left the room. I buried my face in my hands, how could I have let him see me looking like this?

A few minutes later, he came back with a glass of water in his hand. His sleeves were rolled up and I couldn't take my eyes off his strong, tanned forearms. I remembered how it felt to have them wrapped around me in the stock room and felt myself getting hot.

"Drink up" he said, handing me the glass. He kept his eyes on me whilst I drank every last drop.

I wiped my mouth with the back of my hand, "Thanks...for everything."

"I'll be back soon with some food, will you be okay until then?"

"Of course."

He looked at me for a moment as if he was going to say something else but then he turned around and left. I heard the front door open and close behind him.

The hot water felt amazing. I closed my eyes and soaked for a long time before scrubbing my whole body, desperately hoping that it would somehow magically wash away the pain. After getting dry, I felt much better. I scraped my wet hair back into a high ponytail and got changed into my favourite skinny jeans and a comfy cardigan. My head was feeling clearer so I attempted to clean up.

I got butterflies when there was a knock on my door.

Isaac looked even more handsome than before. He was now wearing jeans and a long sleeved t-shirt. He was carrying shopping bags in one hand and some flowers in the other.

"Hi" he said, looking a lot calmer than before.

I opened the door for him, "Hi, come in."

"You smell like strawberries" he said as he followed me into the kitchen.

I blushed, "Oh...it's my shampoo. Sorry you had to see me like that before."

"No rain, no rainbow. These are for you." He handed me a bouquet of lilies and my heart nearly burst.

"Thank you, they're lovely." I inhaled their scent and added lilies to my long mental list of things that I now associated with Isaac.

He smiled, "They always cheer my mother up when she's feeling down."

I filled a vase with water as he started to unpack the shopping bags.

"I've just got you some basics...bread, milk, eggs. They should last you for a couple of days."

I finished arranging the lilies before slowly walking over to him and throwing my arms around his neck. His body was tense at first but then he relaxed and held on to me tight. I buried my face in his chest. "Thank you" I whispered, trying my hardest not to cry again. He held me for a long time and I never wanted to let go. Our body contact was sending electric currents throughout my entire body.

"Um...do you want to stay for a coffee or something?" I asked.

Or something?

"I can't" he replied.

"Oh." I felt a wave of disappointment wash over me.

"I'd like to but I'm meeting somebody in half an hour."

"Oh." I tried my hardest to keep the disappointment off my face.

"It's work related" he blurted out.

"Oh" I replied, because apparently that was my new favourite word. Disappointment was quickly replaced with relief.

"It's actually about you..."

"Me?"

"I'm meeting with Professor Phillips, he's a good friend of mine. I asked him to gather all of the materials that you've missed from this week so that you can catch up before Monday."

Food, flowers and now this? What have I done to deserve this kindness?

"Wow, well thank you. I owe you big time."

"You can buy me a coffee tomorrow."

"Tomorrow?" I asked, a little too enthusiastic.

"I'll need to see you to give you the material. I don't mind going over it with you and passing on any messages from Professor Phillips."

"When?"

"How about ten? At the campus coffee shop?"

Did I really want to step foot in that coffee shop after seeing him and Blondie together in there? I mentally told myself to stop being stupid, it was only a coffee shop. Anyway, this time it would be different, this time he would be with me.

"Okay" I agreed.

"Good."

I nodded, "Good."

A silence passed between us and I swear that there were at least ten elephants in the room. We just continued to look at each other until he spoke, "Okay well I'm going to go. Will you be okay tonight?"

"Yes, I'll be fine."

I walked him to the door and awkwardly waved in his face. Why was I acting like such a loser?

"See you tomorrow."

"Yep, I'll be there" I replied.

His eyes turned dark, "Call me if Lukas shows up."

I rolled mine at him getting all alpha male after just buying me groceries and bringing me flowers, "Okay."

"I mean it, April. Call me."

"I will."

I watched him walk down the path before locking the door behind me.

So life is a rollercoaster, huh? I had a feeling that I was in for one hell of a ride.

Chapter Twenty One

I woke up feeling surprisingly optimistic which was a stark contrast to the past few days. I was slowly beginning to accept that nothing was going to change the past and I needed to focus on the future, starting with my meeting with Isaac in a couple of hours.

I made a special effort with my hair and makeup and couldn't decide if it was brave or stupid of me to wear my red skinny jeans after Isaac had told me that it was his favourite colour.

I practically ran to the coffee shop as I was scared of bumping into Lukas on the way. I couldn't even consider talking to him yet, it was all too raw. I arrived five minutes early and there was no sign of Isaac so I ordered us two cappuccinos and chose a table out of the way, where we could talk privately.

I scowled as I remembered the way Blondie had leant in and whispered in Isaac's ear last week. I wish Katie was still here. I felt bad for not getting in touch with her over the past couple of days but I wasn't ready to talk to anybody about what had happened yet. Except for Isaac.

After a few minutes, I heard some women giggling at a nearby table and looked up to see Isaac walking towards me. The women were staring at him and fanning themselves using their menus. Isaac was oblivious to his little audience and smiled warmly as he sat down opposite me.

"Lovely to see you, as always. How are you feeling today?"

"Better, thanks. Sorry again for yesterday, it's really embarrassing."

"It's called being human and having emotions. As long as you're okay, nothing else matters."

I could feel myself blushing.

"Do you want to talk about what happened?"

I shook my head, it was the last thing that I wanted to do.

"Well if you change your mind, I'm here for you."

"Thanks" I smiled as I handed him his coffee.

"Does this mean that we're quits now and you don't owe me anything?" he asked.

"After yesterday, I think I owe you a lot more than a cup of coffee."

He raised his eyebrow, "Well in that case, you can be my plus one for tonight."

My heart started racing, "What's happening tonight?"

"There's a charity event at Sienna's, a night of live music."

"Sienna's?"

His eyes turned fiery, "Sienna's piano bar...you know, the one with the *stock room*. Don't tell me that you've forgotten about it already."

I blushed, "How could I forget? It's not every day that I get kidnapped."

"I'm pretty sure that you're missing out the most important part of the story."

"Oh yeah, the part where you were being a massive douchebag."

"Is douchebag code for something else?" He gave me a slow, cocky smile which made me all hot and bothered. I was going to be the one fanning myself with the damn menu if he carried on like this.

"Is it appropriate for me to be your plus one?" I asked, ignoring his question.

"I think it's a bit too late to start talking about what's appropriate. But if it makes you feel any better, it's only the same as what we're doing now. We're just two friends who happen to be in the same room as each other."

My heart sank when he used the 'F' word.

"People will see us together" I said.

"Well that usually happens when two people go out together in public."

I sighed, "You know what I mean."

"Look, lots of people are going to be there so they won't even question it. I think you would really enjoy yourself and it's for a good cause, it's not like I'm asking you to go to a strip club with me."

I rolled my eyes, "But what about Blondie?"

Crap, did I just call her that out loud?

"I mean...what about your girlfriend?"

He frowned, "What girlfriend?"

"The blonde woman, the manager of the bar that you're trying to drag me to."

"You mean Abbie? She's not my girlfriend, why would you think that?"

"Oh I don't know, maybe because she had her hands all over you when you were in here last week."

"I knew I should have called you that night." He leant in closer, "April, we're just friends. There's nobody else."

Nobody *else*? Other than who?

"Do all of your friends get to touch you like that?"

"You've got nothing to be jealous of. I still haven't found anyone who can roll around in mud and still look beautiful."

"Oh wow, you're bringing that back up?"

He laughed, "Yep."

"Well at least get it right then. It's *breathtakingly* beautiful."

His eyes twinkled as they burned into mine.

"Anyway, why did she say that she's got a boyfriend but then maul you the next day?"

"Are you stalking me?" he asked.

"That's my line" I replied, once again thinking back to the night of the mixer.

"No, you're supposed to ask me if you look like a stalker. Jeez, at least get it right." He grinned and I couldn't help but laugh.

"Nothing is happening between me and Abbie. You even said it yourself, she's got a boyfriend and it's definitely not me."

"Okay but I still don't think that she'd like it if I rocked up to Sienna's with you."

"I don't care what she likes, I care what you like."

Why did I feel like jumping up and down like a crazy woman?

I cleared my throat and tried to keep my voice level, "Did you bring the lecture notes?"

***

Two hours later, I was completely up to date with all of the work that I had missed. Who knew that catching up on two days' worth of missed work could be fun?

"As much as I've enjoyed your company this morning, I'm not going to have to do this again am I?"

"What, talk to me?" I asked, sarcastically.

"I'm sure we could find something else to do" he quipped back. I shook my head and he grinned, "You're not going to miss any more classes are you?"

"I don't plan on it."

"Good." He stretched before standing up, "Well I better get going, no rest for the wicked. I'll see you tonight."

"Wait, did you not listen to me before? I don't think that it's a good idea." I stood up and watched his eyes shoot down to my jeans before turning fiery.

"*Red* jeans?"

I blushed, forgetting my bold move. "Yes, I've got lots of different colours."

"But you chose to wear your red ones today."

I shrugged and he grinned cockily, "I'll pick you up at seven."

When I didn't respond, he winked at me before walking out of the shop.

Why did I have a feeling that this was the calm before the storm?

***

My mind was consumed with thoughts of Isaac on the way home. I was still feeling pretty smug at his reaction to my jeans. I was considering going shopping for a new dress for tonight when I spotted Dan walking towards me. I groaned and turned around but it was too late.

"April, wait!" He shouted.

I stopped and waited for him to catch up to me. I took a deep breath, preparing for whatever he was about to say.

"How's it going?"

"Great, I've never been better" I replied, sarcastically.

Since Dan had never shown an interest in my feelings, I wondered where this was going.

"Lukas told me everything" he said.

"Then you can probably guess how it's going."

"Have you spoken to him since he left?"

I sighed, "Left where? My house?"

"Oh April, don't you know?" I swear that he was trying his best not to smile, the moron.

"Know what? Just spit it out, Dan."

"He went to Paris to see Madeline."

"Who's Madeline?"

"His fiancée."

My heart sank.

"Sorry, I thought you knew."

"I'm sure you did" I replied.

"He left Thursday morning and he's not back yet."

I didn't want to hear anymore, especially not from Dan. I walked away, trying my best to block out whatever he was shouting after me.

As much as I tried to tell myself that I was okay, I wasn't. It hurt me to know that he had gone to see her the very next morning after seeing me. Why would he go to see her unless he wanted to work things out? Why would he go to Paris, one of the most romantic cities on earth? I took a deep breath, trying my best not to cry.

I looked at my watch and counted how many hours until I got to see Isaac again.

Chapter Twenty Two

When there was a knock on my door at exactly seven, the butterflies in my stomach were almost strong enough to bring me to my knees. I tried to calm myself down before opening the door.

I have always thought that there is something sexy about a man wearing a suit but there are no words to describe Isaac wearing one. It fit him perfectly, highlighting his broad shoulders and athletic frame. He looked so powerful and dominating, I wanted him to dominate me there and then. It drove me wild that his hair was still messy, like there was a part of him that could never be tamed.

I realised that I was staring but it was okay because so was he. His fiery eyes were roaming up and down my body. I was wearing a figure-hugging black dress with my favourite killer heels.

"You look amazing" he said.

"Thanks, you could have made more of an effort" I replied, trying not to laugh.

He raised one eyebrow, "Trust me, it's what's underneath that counts."

"Your shirt?"

He smirked, "Yeah, it's a really nice shirt."

"I bet it is, what does it look like?"

"It's sort of a tan colour."

"Nice."

"I would love to show it you sometime."

"You could always give me a quick flash now before we go."

"What on earth would your neighbours say?" he asked.

"They would probably say that it's a really nice shirt."

I laughed and locked the door behind me.

"No red tonight?" he asked.

I shrugged, "It's what's underneath that counts."

***

After parking up at Sienna's, I held Isaac's hand as he helped me out of his car. His touch sparked something deep inside of me and made my whole body tingle.

He drove a black Porsche which was smooth and sexy just like him. I had tried to act cool and not get too overexcited by all of the different gadgets.

As soon as we stepped into the bar, my eyes darted over to the corridor that led to the toilets...and the stock room. He must have noticed because he started laughing.

It was hard to believe that I was here only a week ago, so much had happened since then. It was busier than I had expected it to be and full of glamorous people sipping champagne. Although I was wearing a nice dress, I felt a little out of place. Isaac hadn't told me how formal it was going to be.

As we made our way over to the bar, Isaac was stopped by at least ten different people. I wondered how he knew all of them but it didn't surprise me because he was so goddamn charming. Most people just said hello and shook his hand but a couple of people had conversations with him. I smiled and nodded politely whilst Isaac did all of the talking. When he stopped to talk to two young women, I caught them eyeing me suspiciously and it made me feel paranoid. Had it been stupid of me to come here tonight?

I was relieved when we finally made it over to the bar. A selection of drinks were already laid out for us. He handed me a glass of champagne before picking up an orange juice for himself.

"Thank you" I said before drinking half of it.

"Thirsty?" he asked.

"Yes, this is really good."

"Only the best for you."

"You're such a sweet talker."

"You love it."

I couldn't argue with that.

"Would you like to sit down? I've reserved a table for us."

"Sounds good."

He led us over to a table which was directly in front of the stage.

"Front row seats, I'm impressed" I said as I sat down.

He grinned, "You don't even want to know what I had to do to get them."

I laughed, "Did you have to show them your amazing shirt?"

"Much worse, I had to show them my lanterns."

I gasped, "And there's me thinking that I'm the only person who gets to see them."

He shook his head, "I swear that there was no touching involved and it didn't mean anything."

I giggled, "That's what they all say."

Out of nowhere, Blondie appeared at our table. Her hair was in loose curls and she was wearing a long silver dress which showed off her perfect hourglass figure.

She placed her hand on Isaac's shoulder, "Zack, I didn't see you arrive."

Zack?

Before I could stop myself, I rolled my eyes. Isaac caught me doing it and cocked his head to one side before smirking.

"Evening, Abbie" he replied.

"New suit?"

He nodded. How the hell does she know whether it's a new suit?

"What do you think of my dress?"

"It's sparkly" he replied.

I had to bite my lip to stop myself from laughing.

"State the obvious why don't you? Anyway, are you nervous?"

Nervous? About what?

"Not at all" he replied, confidently.

She finally decided to acknowledge my existence, turning to look at me. "And who is this?"

"This is April" he said.

I could see straight through her fake smile.

"You look familiar."

Nice to meet you too.

"I was here last weekend, you served me at the bar."

"Oh yeah, I think I remember now. You were with your boyfriend, right?"

"Wrong, he's not my boyfriend."

"He sure looked like your boyfriend."

Well Isaac sure looked like your boyfriend at the coffee shop but apparently it's normal to touch your friends like that.

Isaac looked up at her, "Drop it, Abbie."

She shrugged, "So how do you two know each other?"

"From Uni" I answered.

"Oh, do you work there too?" I could tell by the look on her face that she already knew the answer to that question.

"No."

She narrowed her eyes before looking down at Isaac, "Are you playing with fire, Zack?"

"I'm not playing with anything" he replied bluntly.

There was doubt written all over her face, "Whatever. Are you ready to start?"

"Yes."

She ran her fingers down his arm before walking to the side of the stage.

I raised one eyebrow, "Zack?"

He shook his head, "She knows that I don't like it but she still calls it me anyway."

"Why doesn't that surprise me?"

She tapped the microphone, "Testing, testing, one, two, three."

People began to take their seats and eventually, the room fell quiet.

Abbie cleared her throat, "Good evening Ladies and Gentlemen. I would like to start by thanking you all for coming tonight. As most of you are already aware, this charity is very close to our hearts. With your continued help and support, we are able to help victims of domestic violence and prevent it from happening in the first place."

I joined in with the round of applause.

"You are in for a real treat this evening because we have some of the very best local musicians here to entertain us. To kick the night off, I would like to introduce my good friend, Mr Isaac Sharpe."

My mouth dropped open as my eyes snapped to his. Was this the reason why we had the best seats in the house? The audience began clapping and cheering but I was too shocked to join in. He winked at me before standing up and walking onto the stage. Abbie beamed at him and kissed him on the cheek and I couldn't stop the jealousy from overpowering me.

He sat down in front of the piano before adjusting the

microphone, "Good evening" he purred. That was all it took for the audience to go wild. I waited in anticipation as he stretched his arms out before lightly running his fingers over the keys. I couldn't believe that he hadn't told me he was performing. Is this why Abbie had asked him if he was nervous?

My heart pounded against my chest as I instantly recognised the song that he began to play - *'I won't give up'* by *Jason Mraz*. I was familiar with the lyrics and my mind went into overdrive wondering why he had chosen that particular song. The butterflies in my stomach were fighting to get out as I listened to the beautiful melody that this gorgeous man was creating.

When he started to sing, I completely melted. His voice did things to me that I never thought possible. It was rich and soulful and he oozed confidence. He was completely intoxicating and I didn't ever want to sober up.

During certain parts of the song, he would look straight at me and I knew without a doubt that he had reserved this table so that he could serenade me. I felt every single word that came out of his mouth. He wasn't just singing, he was emoting. I was so close to the stage that it felt like I was up there with him. Although the room was full, it felt like it was just me and him.

As the song progressed, he put even more emotion into it and by the final note, I had tears in my eyes. The audience burst into applause and without thinking, I stood up and began clapping like a crazy woman.

He thanked the audience before standing up and taking a bow. Abbie walked back on stage and hugged him before introducing the next singer. I didn't hear a word that she was saying because I was focusing all of my attention on Isaac. When he sat back down, I was speechless. I felt like we had just shared a special moment and I didn't want to say or do something that might ruin it.

His eyes were full of emotion as he leant in closer to me, "What did you think?"

"I loved it. I can't believe you didn't tell me that you were performing."

He shrugged, "It was a last minute thing."

"You were amazing."

"Were? Don't you mean *are*?" His eyes danced playfully.

"What you *are* is an arrogant jerk. Just one who can sing and play the piano really well." I couldn't keep the grin off my face.

We fell into a pattern of watching the other performers before Isaac would turn to me and tell me all about them. I tried to listen to him as best as I could but my mind was consumed with images of him singing to me. I kept running the lyrics over and over in my head like a lunatic until I couldn't take it anymore.

"Isaac, why did you choose to sing that song?" I asked.

"It's a nice song."

"That's my point."

He laughed, "Do you want me to sing a heavy metal song next time?"

"You know what I mean."

"No I don't, I think you should say what's on your mind."

I narrowed my eyes at him, he wasn't making this easy on me. "Well the lyrics are pretty deep, it sounded like you really meant what you were singing."

"I meant every word."

Welcome back, butterflies.

I wanted to be direct with him and say what was on my mind. I wanted to ask him if he had reserved this table on purpose so that he could sing to me. I wanted to ask him if he was actually singing about not giving up on *us*. I wanted to ask him whether there was any truth in the lyrics, especially the parts where he sang about waiting and giving somebody space to figure things out. But instead, I just sat there with my mouth closed. I was too scared. Or maybe I already knew the answers.

I looked away when the intensity of his eyes threatened to make me spontaneously combust. We didn't discuss it any further but it was on my mind for the rest of the evening. I purposely slowed down on the champagne to stop myself from blurting out something stupid.

After the final performer had left the stage, I stood up.

"You don't waste any time do you?" Isaac asked.

"I'm going to the ladies room."

He raised an eyebrow and smiled at me seductively.

"You're not going to follow me this time are you?" I asked.

"Follow you? I don't know what you're talking about, maybe you should jog my memory?"

"Maybe you should get lost."

He laughed as I shook my head and walked away. My body temperature sky rocketed as I passed the stock room.

On my way back to the table, I groaned when I saw Abbie talking to Isaac. I wonder if she would jump into my grave just as quick?

As I got closer, it looked like they were having some sort of heated discussion. I debated whether I should give them some space but in all honesty, I didn't want her to spend any more time with him. They stopped talking when they saw me approach.

"Don't stop on my account" I told them.

"Oh, we won't" Abbie replied in the bitchiest tone imaginable.

I laughed at her response.

"What's so funny?" she asked.

"You, actually."

"Abbie" Isaac warned.

"Why is she laughing at me?"

Isaac ignored her and turned to me, "Are you ready to leave?"

"Ready when you are" I replied.

"Then let's go."

Abbie let out a dramatic sigh before stalking off.

"What's her problem?" I asked as we made our way to the exit.

"She's had too much to drink" he replied as he waved goodbye to some people.

"Then what was her excuse at the start of the evening?"

He smirked as he held the door open for me.

I squealed as I stepped out into the rain and tried to cover my hair using my tiny handbag. It really was a pathetic excuse for a bag, fitting only my keys and lipstick inside. The rain was bouncing and some of the roads were beginning to flood. Isaac laughed at me before grabbing hold of my hand and leading us to the car park around the back of the building. I tried my best not to step in any puddles but it was difficult when all that I could concentrate on was how smooth Isaac's hand felt.

When we were both in the car, he shook the rain out of his hair and it drove me wild. I was staring at him open-mouthed like a mad woman and I had to stop myself from reaching out and running my fingers through it. Just when I thought that I couldn't take anymore, he took his suit jacket off and wrapped it around my shoulders.

"Thank you" I mumbled whilst drooling at his muscles through his tight fitting shirt, "You're right, by the way."

"About what?" he asked.

"It *is* a very nice shirt."

He grinned as he brought the car to life, "It's all yours if you want it."

Kill me now.

When I didn't reply, he looked at me with playful eyes, "Do you want it?"

Like you wouldn't believe.

I laughed, "You really want to give it to me, don't you? You're such a shirt whore."

He laughed, "Guilty as charged."

Even though it sent my head in a spin every time, I loved our playful banter.

"I love the rain" he announced as we got onto the main road.

My eyes widened, "Are you crazy?"

He grinned, "Probably. Nothing bad ever happens when it rains."

I frowned but couldn't keep from smiling, "Where have you got that crazy theory from?"

"My brain."

"Ah see, that's the problem."

Our conversation stayed light-hearted until we pulled up outside my house. I suddenly wished that I lived further away. He turned the engine off and it was silent apart from the rain beating down. The weather forecasters had predicted showers but this was more of a downpour. In that moment, it felt like we were in our own little bubble just watching the world go by.

"Did you have fun tonight?" he asked.

"I did, thank you."

"What did you think of the music?"

"It was awesome apart from that first musician, he was a little creepy."

He grinned, "Well it didn't help that there was a creepy girl sat in the front row."

I laughed but stopped when he reached out and placed his hand on top of mine.

"I'm glad that you're smiling, it hurt me to see you so upset. I would do anything to go back in time and take the pain away."

I looked down at his hand which was gently stroking mine. I began to think about fate and how I wouldn't be sitting here right now if everything with Lukas hadn't happened the way it had. Although I was still hurting, maybe it had happened for a reason. Maybe I was exactly where I was supposed to be.

I had a moment of realisation where everything seemed to become clear in my head. There was a reason why my heart was beating like this. There was a reason why I had butterflies in my stomach whenever Isaac was around. There was a reason why I was sat in his car at this exact moment. How much longer was I willing to fight my true feelings? Did I really want to go through life having regrets and wondering what might have been?

I turned to look at him and the intensity of his stare made me light headed. I loved the way that he looked at me like I was the only girl in the world. I could feel the electricity between us, even stronger than the night that we first met. This was the moment.

I leant in, desperately wanting to feel his lips on mine. However, nothing could have prepared me for what happened next.

He backed away.

"April...I can't..." his voice was unsteady.

My eyes widened in shock as confusion, betrayal and anger washed over me. Tears filled my eyes as I desperately tried to make sense of what was happening.

Was this one big game for him? Was it only ever about the chase? I shrugged out of his jacket.

"Can't or won't?" I spat in reply before storming out of the car and running to my front door.

Once inside, I locked the door behind me and sank to the floor. I buried my face in my hands, still in complete shock. It had taken me weeks to find the strength to follow my heart and now that I have, he tells me that he *can't*? So he can take me out of classes, warn other men to stay away from me and pull me into stock rooms but now he *can't?*

But what about the song? He had even admitted that he meant every word that he sang. I was so confused, I couldn't even think straight.

My heart stopped when I heard a knock on the door. I stood up and opened it to see Isaac staring back at me. The image of him frozen to the spot in the pouring rain would be etched into my memory forever. Droplets of rain were running down his face, giving the illusion that he was crying. Only, the fine line between illusion and reality was quickly becoming blurred. My eyes moved down to his shirt which was now completely see through. The adrenaline pumped through me as I was transfixed by his six pack. I wanted to touch him. Hell, I wanted to touch myself.

This was undoubtedly a cross roads moment. I knew that whatever was going to happen next would change everything.

He closed his eyes and tilted his head back, letting the rain wash over him. I held my breath as I watched him. When he opened his eyes, the passion in them was unmistakable but then again, so was the fear. He slowly took a step towards me and it was the sign that I had been waiting for. I copied him and within seconds, I was drenched. His eyes widened in response before turning dark.

He closed the gap between us, crushing his wet body against mine. The contact sent a jolt of electricity through me, awakening all of my senses. He took my hand and held it against his chest, "Feel that? It beats for you."

His hands grabbed my behind as he lifted me up, urging my legs to wrap around his waist. He looked deep into my soul as he leant in to kiss me. I had waited so long for this moment, to touch him, to taste him. When our lips finally met, I knew that my life had been changed forever. It would never be complete without him in it.

I felt like I was being kissed for the very first time all over again. His lips were soft yet strong and the anticipation of what might happen next was almost too much to handle. I ran my fingers through his hair and tugged on it which made him groan in response. He pulled away and looked at me with fiery eyes whilst I tried to steady my breathing. Only then did I realise that we were still outside. A small part of me panicked in case somebody had seen us but when I looked into Isaac's eyes, it made me realise that he was worth the risk.

"We need to get out of these wet clothes" he almost growled.

"Inside" I told him.

I could feel him growing hard against me as he carried me inside and didn't stop until we were in my bedroom. He stopped at the edge of the bed before letting go. I squealed as my back hit the bed, missing his touch already.

His eyes burned into mine as he took off his shoes before slowly unbuttoning his wet shirt. After purposely taking his time with it, he let it drop to the floor and I gasped at the sight in front of me. Not only was his body even hotter than I had imagined but he had several tattoos across his chest.

He laughed, "Should I take that as a compliment?"

I nodded as I stared open-mouthed at the large cross with the letter 'S' inside. He also had stars and musical notes surrounding it. He just kept getting hotter and hotter.

I sat up so that I was eye level with his abs. He had the most unbelievable six pack and if I didn't touch it soon, I was going to explode. I edged towards him and wrapped my arms around his waist before kissing his bare skin. He groaned which turned me on even more. He stroked my hair and watched as the kissing quickly escalated into licking. My tongue explored the hard, deep ridges of his abdominal muscles before moving lower down to taste his V lines. When he couldn't take anymore, he pushed me back and climbed on top of me.

"I want you so bad" he said as he pulled my dress up and over my head in less than two seconds. "Fuck me" he said as he stared at my red lacy underwear.

"That's the plan" I replied, trying to look as seductive as possible.

He leaned back to get a better look at me, "You're keeping those heels on."

191

I pulled him back on top of me and he kissed me with even more ferocity. I sucked on his lower lip whilst unzipping his trousers, pushing them down as far as they would go. He rested his arms on either side of my head and pushed against the bed, lifting his body up so that I could take them off completely. I tugged on his boxer shorts and took them off along with his trousers so that he was naked. He was perfect from head to toe and I wanted him inside me.

I loved the feel of his hot, smooth body against mine. He kissed me even harder, his hands exploring every part of my body before unhooking my bra and peeling it off. Next, his hands moved down my body, gripping my knickers and pulling them off. I gasped as his fingers entered me and got lost in a sea of pleasure. I was completely at his mercy but before I got too carried away, I leant over and opened my bedside drawer, retrieving a foil packet. Isaac took it off me and ripped it open with his teeth. He looked so goddamn sexy with rain still dripping from his hair.

He grabbed hold of my legs whilst lining his body up with mine. I had dreamt about this moment for weeks and now it was finally happening. How had I ever thought that this was wrong when it felt so right?

He kissed me gently this time before slowly pushing into me. He completely took my breath away. It started out slow and steady until he increased the pace, rocking against me over and over again. Our kisses alternated between slow and gentle to fast and greedy.

I looked him in the eye and felt overwhelmed with emotion. I was crazy about this man. I could feel the hot pressure starting to swell inside me so urged him in deeper. Within seconds, my eyes rolled back into my head and I was crying out his name. My body shuddered as I rode the wave of pleasure that was taking over me. He carried on pushing into me until his body tensed up and he groaned in his own pleasure. He slowed his breathing before lying down next to me and pulling me into his side.

I was exhausted in the best possible way and couldn't keep the huge smile off my face.

Sometimes you don't realise how lost you really were until you find your way back home. Isaac was my home.

He held me tight whilst stroking my hair and before long, I was fast asleep.

***

I panicked when I woke up and heard somebody in the house. I sat up and spotted the wet clothes strewn on the floor.

So it wasn't a dream after all.

Memories of last night flashed through my mind and I did a little dance. I was happier than I had been in a long time.

I put on some fresh clothes before sneaking into the bathroom to wash my face and brush my teeth. After tying my hair up in a messy bun, I went back into the bedroom to pick up the wet clothes before going to see Isaac.

When I found him in the kitchen, my eyes nearly popped out of my head. He was making breakfast wearing only his boxer shorts. He had his back to me and I could easily stare at his perfect body all day.

"What's cooking?" I asked as I went and put the clothes into the dryer.

He turned around and smiled, "Good morning sleeping beauty, I hope you like pancakes." The front view was even better than the back.

"What kind of silly question is that? I love pancakes."

"How are you feeling today?" he asked.

"I'm good, you?"

"Better than ever."

I grinned, "Should we talk about last night?"

"About how awesome it was?"

I laughed, "About anything."

"If you want to. All I know is that I want you to fall asleep in my arms every night."

He made me feel warm and fuzzy inside. I wanted the same thing more than anything and I really hoped that we could find a way to be together. I couldn't take any more heart break and I definitely couldn't take getting kicked off the course.

"I thought you might regret what happened and run off in the middle of the night" I said, half joking.

"I couldn't, my clothes were still wet."

He laughed when I scowled at him.

"Of course I wouldn't run away, I'm right where I want to be."

I grinned as I watched the way his muscles moved when he flipped the pancakes over. I would never be able to look at them in the same way again.

"Can I ask you something?"

"Of course" he replied.

"Why did you pull away from me in the car?"

"I was scared that you were rushing into it."

"Rushing into it? I think I've done the complete opposite, I've had weeks to think about it."

"I meant rushing into something so soon after Lukas. I just needed to know that you were sure first."

"I'm sure."

I hadn't even thought about it like that. Did he think that he was some kind of rebound for me? If only he knew how many nights that I had dreamt about being with him. A dream that had now come true.

***

After stuffing our faces with pancakes, I moaned when he put his dry clothes back on. Why did I even put them in the dryer in the first place?

He laughed, "Can I come and see you tomorrow night?"

I grinned, "It's a date."

He cupped my face in his hands and stared down at me with his piercing blue eyes, "That's my line, remember?"

He was so beautiful, he almost took my breath away. "I remember" I whispered.

"I've waited too long for that date" he said.

"Me too."

He kissed me before pulling me into his chest. God, he smelt so good.

"I wish that I could spend today with you but I've got some meetings that I can't get out of."

"It's okay, I'm sure I can wait until tomorrow night."

"I'm not going to be able to stop thinking about you, it's going to drive me crazy."

"Crazy is good" I said without thinking, finally understanding what Katie meant.

Katie. I forgot to call her last night before Isaac picked me up. I made a mental note to call her as soon as possible.

"Well in that case, I'm batshit crazy" he replied. "Are you going to be okay going back to class tomorrow?"

I shrugged, "I've got to get on with it."

"If he starts giving you any hassle or upsets you, come and see me straight away."

He left me with a kiss that I wouldn't be forgetting anytime soon.

I walked him to the door and then watched as he got into his car and drove off.

What a difference a day makes.

I found my phone and turned it on for the first time since

Wednesday. I ignored all of the missed calls and texts, trying to forget about the past and just concentrate on the future. I dialled Katie's number and she answered immediately, "Where the fuck have you been?"

I decided to take a leaf out of her book and scrap the greeting. Instead, I sighed happily, "I'm going to marry that boy one day."

Chapter Twenty Three

I felt a mix of emotions when I woke up on Monday morning. I was excited at the thought of spending more time with Isaac but nervous to see Lukas in class. I missed our friendship but I wasn't sure if I could ever forgive him after what he did. He had betrayed me the whole time and it would take a lot to trust him again, even as a friend. I didn't have a clue what I was going to say or do.

A few of Katie's suggestions from yesterday popped into my head but they all resulted in me getting arrested so I scrapped them. I had spent most of yesterday afternoon answering hundreds of her questions and of course, she wanted to know every tiny detail about my night with Isaac. She was flabbergasted by what Lukas had done and offered to bury him under her patio. But she soon forgot about all of that when the discussion turned to Isaac.

I took a deep breath before walking into my first lecture. I quickly glanced around and felt relief wash over me when I didn't see Lukas anywhere. Lucy waved at me so I went and sat down next to her.

"How are you?" she asked, giving me a sympathetic smile.

"I'm doing good, thanks."

"I'm sorry to hear about you and Lukas, I never thought that he would do something like that. He seemed like he was completely in love with you."

I shrugged.

"It must be tough" she added.

"I just don't want it to be awkward in class."

"Well he's not back yet so don't worry."

"Back from where, Paris?"

"Yeah, Dan said that he's not been back since he left last week."

"So what have you been up to?" I asked, trying to steer the conversation in a different direction. She proceeded to tell me all about her weekend but I didn't hear a word that she said. Even though

I wanted to be with Isaac, it still hurt me to hear that Lukas wasn't back. Above everything else, he was supposed to be my friend but it didn't feel like he was even trying. Maybe it was easier this way, that we both move on and leave our friendship in the past.

I decided to put it to the back of my mind and concentrate on my lessons as best as I could. It helped that I wasn't nervous about bumping into Lukas around campus. I was tempted to go and see Isaac on my free period but I couldn't start being reckless now, not when something was actually happening between us. I was still scared that somebody was going to find out and we would both get kicked out of the university but being sensible hadn't worked out all that great for me so it was time to try a different approach. To be honest, I didn't even know what was happening between us. All I know is that I'm crazy about him and want to spend more time with him. I know that he cares about me but I don't know if he wants more. Is it even possible to have more?

So instead of being reckless, I spent my lunch hour in the library. I giggled when I walked past one of the 'nerds' that Katie had tried to flirt with when she had come to visit. I was up to date with coursework so logged onto the computers. After checking my emails only to find an empty inbox, I went on a gossip website instead. Half an hour well spent.

As soon as my last lecture had finished, I was excited to go home and start planning what to wear to see Isaac.

As I walked past the coffee shop, I heard somebody shout my name. I turned around to see Abbie approaching me. I was pretty sure that she wasn't about to buy me a blueberry muffin.

"It's April, right?"

"Right."

She nodded, "Did you enjoy yourself on Saturday night, April?"

"I thoroughly enjoyed myself, thank you." I wasn't referring to my night at Sienna's.

"In case you failed to notice, Isaac is a very good friend of mine and has been for a long time now. I'd do anything to stop him from getting hurt."

"That's sweet of you but why are you telling me this?"

"Because I know that you're up to something and based on the fact that he brought you to Sienna's when he knows that you're a student tells me that he's actually falling for your plan."

"And what plan would that be?"

"I've not figured it out yet, maybe you're after his money or you're trying to get good grades but I'm warning you to stay away from him."

I was quickly getting tired of the bullshit that was spewing from her mouth.

"*You* need to stay away from *me*." I turned and tried to walk away but she grabbed hold of my arm. I shrugged her off, "Don't you dare touch me again."

"Look, you're not the first student to have a crush on him and you certainly won't be the last. I just wonder when you're going to realise that he's not interested in little girls. Do you really think that he would throw his career away for someone like you?"

Now she was getting me really angry.

"Does your boyfriend know that you're warning me to stay away from another man?"

"My boyfriend knows that I do whatever I want, whenever I want."

"Well that sounds like a healthy relationship. Maybe you should spend more time with him and less time pining over Isaac and threatening *little girls*."

I had to walk away from her before I flipped out. I couldn't believe her nerve, how dare she try to warn me off him like that? My relationship with Isaac had nothing to do with her. I took some deep breaths and counted to ten. When I got home, instead of wasting any more time thinking about Abbie, I focused on my evening with Isaac, away from the rest of the world.

***

When Isaac turned up just after eight, I was giddy with excitement as I opened the door. He was wearing jeans and a plain grey t-shirt which of course showed off his perfect physique. He could probably wear a sack and still look jaw-droppingly hot.

He leant down and gave me a heart stopping kiss which was definitely worth the wait. His lips were even softer and more delicious than I had remembered.

He handed me a gift bag, "This is for you."

I grinned, "A present? You shouldn't have."

He watched as I looked inside and took out a little bonsai tree. My heart melted at the thought behind it.

"I love it."

He grinned, "I wanted you to have a little reminder of our night under the tree."

"Wait...where are the lanterns?"

"Don't push your luck."

I laughed, "It's perfect, thank you so much."

I threw my arms around him before taking his hand and leading him into the living room. I placed the bonsai tree in the middle of the coffee table before sitting down on the sofa. Isaac brought my legs up so that they were resting across his lap. I beamed at such a simple gesture.

"I'm not sure if we're going to be able to fit underneath it but we could try" I said, still looking at the tiny tree.

He laughed, "So how has your day been? I've not stopped thinking about you."

My cheeks were beginning to ache from smiling so much, "It was okay, Lukas wasn't in any classes."

"Maybe he's too ashamed to show his face."

"No, he's in Paris with his fiancée or ex-fiancée, I don't even know."

"Oh, have you spoken to him?" I could tell that he was trying to stay as nonchalant as possible.

"No, not since he left my house last week. I wouldn't even know what to say to him."

"I know what I'd say to him, it involves a few swear words. I'd tell him that he's a complete idiot for losing the best thing to ever happen to him. But you know what? He's got to live with that for the rest of his life, if that's not punishment enough then I don't know what is."

I smiled, his words meant a lot to me.

"How was your day?" I asked.

"Busy. It doesn't help that Abbie has decided to start acting the fool."

I groaned when he mentioned her name, "Have you seen her today? She caught up with me on my way home."

He sighed, "Yes, I've heard."

"So she told you?"

"She mentioned that she saw you but didn't go in to detail."

"No, she wouldn't. I'm guessing she left out the part where she threatened me to stay away from you?"

"She definitely left that part out. I'm sorry, I've told her to back off."

"What's her problem?"

"She *is* the problem. There are a lot of things that you don't know about me, April. Things that have happened in the past. I don't want to upset you but I think it's important that you know about some of those things."

I nodded as a knot formed in my stomach.

"Me and Abbie used to be intimate."

I felt sick, I didn't want to imagine Isaac being intimate with anybody else.

"How long ago?"

I held my breath, praying to god that it wasn't recent.

"A couple of months ago, I didn't even know you then."

I nodded as relief flooded through me.

"No wonder she's warning me to stay away from you then. Was it serious?"

"No, it was only ever a casual thing."

"For both of you?"

"Yes, she knew what it was. No feelings were involved."

"I think she's broken that part of the contract."

He nodded.

"How long were you casual for?"

"About a year on and off."

My eyes widened, "A year? Why did it never turn into something serious?"

"Because none of us wanted it to. I wasn't interested in a relationship with her."

I nodded, "I can see why, I'm expecting to find a horse's head in my bed soon."

He laughed, "I'm sorry that I didn't tell you the other night. I didn't think it was important but now that she's being difficult, it's important that you know what happened between us."

"Has she tried to sleep with you recently?"

"Yes."

"And you said no?"

"Of course, I'm not interested anymore."

"So she wants you but can't have you and she thinks it's because of me."

He nodded, "She's jealous of you. I've had to tell her that you're my student and nothing more for obvious reasons but she's not buying it."

"How long have you known her?"

His face turned solemn, "A long time, she was my sister's best friend."

"Was?"

He nodded, "Will you come for a little drive with me?"

"A drive? Where to?"

"You'll see."

Chapter Twenty Four

I was confused when we pulled into the car park at Sienna's.

"Isaac, what are we doing here?" I asked as he helped me out of his car.

"I want to show you something."

"I don't think it's a good idea coming here, I don't want to make things worse with Abbie."

"Just trust me."

We walked around to the front entrance before he tried opening the door.

"Oh that's a shame, it's closed."

I pointed to the opening times, "Closed on Mondays and Tuesdays." I was relieved that we wouldn't be running into Abbie after all.

He held his car keys up, "It's a good job that I've got this then."

"What, a car?"

He smirked as he unlocked the door.

I narrowed my eyes, "Why have you got a key for this place?"

When we stepped inside, he punched a code into the alarm system before flicking the lights on.

I laughed, "Of course you know the alarm code too..."

I watched him as he walked behind the bar and poured himself a glass of orange juice.

"Would you like a drink?" he asked.

I shook my head but couldn't keep the smile off my face, "Would you like to tell me what's going on?"

He walked back around the bar and sat on one of the stools, pulling another out for me. I sat down and looked at him expectantly.

"I know the owner" he said.

"You must know them pretty well for you to have a key."

"I do...he's awesome."

I wiggled my eyebrows up and down, "You'll have to introduce us some time."

He laughed, "You already know him."

"Do I?"

"You're looking at him."

My eyes widened, "Are you joking?"

"No."

"You own this place?"

"Yep."

"Wow, you kept that one quiet."

He laughed, "Sorry, I wasn't trying to keep it a secret or anything."

"Well I thought it might have come up when you invited me to the charity evening."

"I didn't want you to say yes just because you felt obliged."

"So how long have you had this place?"

"Two years."

"I'm impressed, you've done a great job."

He grinned, "Thanks."

"Can I ask you something?"

"Of course."

"Why do you still have a job at the university if you own this place?"

He sighed, "Trust me, that's all I've been asking myself these past few weeks. I've always enjoyed working there, it's where me and my sister both studied so I have lots of fond memories."

I nodded. "Why did you make Abbie the manager?"

"Although she's a pain in the ass, she *is* a good manager."

"You said that she used to be your sister's best friend?"

His eyes turned sad which made me wonder what had happened between them.

"It's okay, we don't have to talk about it" I told him.

"No...I want to."

I held his hand and began to gently stroke it.

"I named this bar after my sister."

"Sienna."

He nodded, "She was my best friend. We were so close growing up, people thought that we were twins because we went everywhere together and even used to wear the same clothes. I'm a year older than her so she found it difficult when I moved over here to study but a year later she followed in my footsteps. I'd walk her to class in the morning and we used to have the same group of friends. Everything was going great until she started dating this guy. He seemed okay at first but after a few months he got really possessive and tried to stop her from seeing me and her friends. One night, they had a big argument and I ended up breaking his nose."

"Good on you" I said as I continued to stroke his hand reassuringly.

"She didn't talk to me for a couple of weeks afterwards but then I apologised and everything went back to normal. I tried to tell her more than once that he was no good for her but she didn't want to hear it. A few weeks later, just before we broke up for summer, he threw all of her make-up in the bin. That's when she finally saw him for what he was. She broke up with him and we didn't hear from him after that."

He took a deep breath and I could see how difficult this was for him.

"It was a couple of weeks after my graduation. I was travelling abroad and she was at home visiting our parents. One day, my parents were out and he turned up at the house. The neighbours heard a lot of shouting and screaming."

Tears began to roll down his cheeks and even though I was trying to stay strong, I couldn't hold them back. It destroyed me to see him this way.

"My parents came home to find their only daughter fighting for her life on the kitchen floor. She died on the way to the hospital. That was the worst day of my life and I can't tell you how it felt to get that phone call. I blamed it all on myself. I should have been there for her, I should have done more than break his nose that day. I got on the next flight home and searched everywhere for him. I was going to kill him with my bare hands and I didn't even care that I would go to prison. The fucking police got to him first. A minimum of thirty years in prison isn't good enough for me, he took my sisters life so he should lose his."

"I'm so sorry, Isaac. Nobody should have to go through that." I wrapped my arms around him and rocked him like a baby whilst we both cried. It devastated me that there was nothing I could do to ease his pain.

Eventually, he took a deep breath and sat back up, "I miss her every single day. She was such an amazing person, you would have loved her."

"She sounds amazing just like her brother."

He smiled, "She was a musician too and we always dreamt about opening our own piano bar so with the help of my Dad, I did it for her."

I swallowed the lump in my throat, "She would be so proud of you."

"Thank you" he whispered. "My parents sold the house and moved away and I came back here. Even though it hurts, I'm surrounded by so many wonderful memories. Some days, it feels like she's still here with me."

I nodded, "Is the tree for Sienna?"

"Kind of. I started going to write there after she died, it really helped me channel my emotions. I began lighting the candles for her and I've just carried on ever since."

I smiled and remembered what he had said when we had been sat underneath it. I was the only person who he had taken there and it made my heart swell.

Hearing him talk about his sister put everything into perspective for me and made me realise what was important. Life is too precious to waste.

"Abbie was Sienna's best friend back at home. When she died, she blamed herself just like I did. She said that best friends were supposed to protect each other. Her parents were really worried about her and asked me if she could come and spend some time with me over here. She stayed in my spare room for a few weeks and then started working at the bar. She eventually rented a place of her own and she's not been back home since. I'm only telling you this because I want to be honest with you."

"I understand" I replied.

"In the beginning, we were both in a lot of pain and we ended up sleeping together to try and find some comfort. As time went on, I used it as a kind of escape from reality but I've never felt anything more for her. She actually used to be really shy but now she's turned into a really bitter, untrusting person because of what happened to Sienna. She won't allow herself to get too close to a man and always ends up sabotaging her relationships. I think she feels like we've got a special bond because of what we've been through."

I nodded, "That makes sense."

Although Abbie had no excuse for acting like a total bitch, I started to understand why she acted the way that she did. Perhaps she really was just trying to protect Isaac and of course, I couldn't tell her how I really felt about him because of our situation.

"She's still out of order for threatening you. I've considered asking her to find a new job but in all honesty, I don't trust her. I think it's safer to keep her exactly where I can see her."

"What do you mean?"

"She's very manipulative. I think she can tell that I like you and I wouldn't be surprised if she tried to cause some trouble for us. So for the time being, I'm trying to keep on her good side."

"Good thinking."

He nodded and pulled me into his arms, "Thanks for listening and understanding, you don't know how much it means to me."

"I'm just glad that you trust me enough to talk to me about it, I know how difficult that was for you."

"It's getting late, do you want to stay over at mine tonight? I've got a spare toothbrush."

I tried not to jump up and down with excitement. I wanted to spend the night with him more than anything. I wanted to fall asleep in his arms listening to the sound of his steady heartbeat and wake up next to him in the morning.

"I would love that. I've got class in the morning though."

He walked over to the door and locked it before taking my hand and leading me around the other side of the bar.

"I thought we were going to your house?" I asked.

"We are" he replied as we walked through a door that led into a private area. Straight ahead were some staff toilets along a corridor that led to a fire escape. But to our left was a staircase which we started to climb. The penny finally dropped.

"You live here?" I asked, more shocked than I probably should have been.

"Yep."

"So that's why you were here the night you kidnapped me."

He shrugged, "I saw you on the CCTV cameras but you already know that I'm a stalker."

I laughed, "Wow, you're taking the whole stalker thing seriously."

"If a jobs worth doing, it's worth doing well."

"No wonder you came out of nowhere that night and didn't have a problem dragging me into the stock room."

He laughed as he unlocked his front door.

"I bet you don't get any sleep up here with the music playing all the time."

He raised one eyebrow, "It's got sound proofing."

"Interesting" I said, with a huge grin on my face.

Chapter Twenty Five

I floated through the next day with a permanent smile on my face. After Isaac had taken me back home in the morning, I had just enough time to get changed and grab my books before walking to class. Lukas was still nowhere to be seen which meant that nothing was going to dampen my mood today. Lucy picked up on the fact that I was in an especially good mood but I just grinned and nodded.

When I got home, I had a bath and then rang Katie to tell her about last night.

"So let me get this straight...he's hot, good in bed *and* he owns his own bar? Jackpot!"

"I really hope I don't get kicked off the course, because that's going to happen before I stop seeing Isaac."

"Seriously, have you had a personality transplant or something? You sound like a completely different person" she said.

"I don't think I have, maybe I should check for a scar though. I'm just tired of hiding my true feelings, life's too short."

"I've been telling you that for years."

I laughed, "Wait, somebody's at the door."

"Who is it?"

"Give me chance, woman. I'm not expecting anyone."

I opened the door and grinned when I saw Isaac staring back at me.

"I miss you already" he said.

My knees went weak as Katie squealed down the phone.

"Come in" I told him. He smiled and closed the door behind him.

"Is that him? Oh my god, can I speak to him?" I heard Katie shouting.

"I've got to go, I'll ring you tomorrow."

"Drop me like a sack of spuds why don't you?"

"Okay, bye" I laughed as I hung up on her.

"So you miss me, do you?" I asked before leaning up and giving him a kiss to rival all other kisses.

"Mmmhmm" he murmured against my lips.

My body tingled as the adrenaline pumped through my veins. He pushed me against the wall and parted my legs with one of his before pressing his body in between my thighs. He fit perfectly like the missing puzzle piece of a jigsaw. My hands explored his hard body as the kiss became even more intense. Our tongues teased one another as I lifted his arms up and pulled his t-shirt off. I threw it onto the floor before leaning down and kissing his hot, bare chest. I squealed when he suddenly threw me over his shoulder and carried me into the bedroom. When my feet touched the floor again, I pushed him onto the bed and climbed on top of him.

I wasted no time as I pulled down the zipper on his jeans. It was quickly becoming one of my favourite sounds. He pulled the foil packet out of his jeans pocket before lifting his body up with me still straddling him so that I could pull his jeans and pants off.

"You love getting me naked" he said.

"You're stating the obvious with that one" I replied as I ripped open the foil packet before rolling the condom onto him. He growled and pulled me flat against his body before flipping me over so that he was on top.

"That feels a million times better when you do it" he said.

He pulled my pyjama bottoms down before slowly running his fingers up the inside of my thighs. When his fingers reached my knickers, he pulled them to one side whilst kissing my neck. I gasped in surprise when he thrust into me. He kissed me hard like he was claiming me and I was more than happy to be claimed by him.

My hands explored his muscular back and he seemed to like it when I dug my nails into his shoulder blades, making him thrust harder. Within minutes, I could feel the hot pressure already starting to build inside of me.

"You feel so good" he whispered, "I love being inside you." That was enough to push me over the edge. The pleasure heightened until my body couldn't take anymore and I exploded around him, my entire body tingling. He stopped kissing me and watched me writhe around underneath him which in turn prolonged my pleasure. I called out his name as he carried on thrusting into me. I could feel the pressure starting to climb again, this time much faster. I squeezed my eyes shut, a virgin to this kind of pleasure.

"Do you want me to stop?" he asked.

"Don't you dare."

He laughed and picked up the pace before making my body shudder once more. I bit my lip to stop myself from screaming.

He slowed down and within seconds, he found his own release. I felt his whole body tense up as he called out my name. He grinned and wrapped his arms around me, "I want to make you happy."

"You just did...twice" I replied.

He held my face in his hands, "That's not enough, it will never be enough. I want to make you happy from now until forever."

I took a deep breath to try and calm the butterflies, "I want that too."

He looked at me with eyes full of love and it felt like my heart was going to burst.

We held each other for a long time until he eventually drifted off to sleep. I really needed to use the bathroom so I wriggled out from underneath him. He woke up and smiled at me, looking totally happy and relaxed, "Are you okay?" he asked.

"I'm more than okay. I'm just going to the bathroom and to make us a drink."

"Okay beautiful."

I grinned as I put on my dressing gown. After using the bathroom, I headed to the kitchen to make us a drink. Whilst the kettle was boiling, I thought that I heard somebody knocking on the front door. When I went to check, I froze when I saw who was standing in front of me.

"Lukas" I whispered.

"Hello April."

I was completely caught off guard and didn't know what to say or do. We stared at each other for a long time before I tightened the belt on my dressing gown.

"What...why...what..." I mumbled, having lost the ability to form a proper sentence.

"Can I talk to you?" he asked.

I closed my eyes and tried to get my head together, "Now's not a good time."

My heart stopped when I heard Isaac's voice coming up behind me and before I could even attempt to stop what was about to happen, he walked into the hallway and straight into view of Lukas. Like me, Isaac froze before his eyes snapped to mine. I watched as all traces of happiness drained from them in a matter of seconds. There was no way that we could talk ourselves out of this one...Isaac was only wearing his boxer shorts.

I sighed and turned to face Lukas who was looking between me and Isaac like he was watching a game of tennis.

"I think you'd better come in" I said.

"I thought that now wasn't a good time?"

"We don't want any trouble" added Isaac.

"Well you're not exactly making an effort to stay out of trouble are you, Mr Sharpe?" He made a point of emphasising the 'Mr'.

"You're in no position to talk about staying out of trouble so why don't you come in and we can discuss this like adults?" Isaac replied.

"Can you at least put some trousers on?" Lukas asked as he stepped into the hall.

Isaac looked at me whilst bending down to pick his t-shirt up off the floor. When I nodded, he turned and walked towards the bedroom.

"What are you doing, April? This is crazy. What if somebody finds out?" Lukas whispered.

"Then I'll have to deal with it just like I had to deal with finding out that you were engaged."

I could see the pain in his eyes, "I'm so sorry for hurting you. I needed to talk to you one last time before you shut me out of your life completely."

"Who says that I haven't already?"

"Well have you?"

I sighed, "No, come and sit down."

He followed me into the living room and we both sat down on the sofa. It hurt when I thought back to happier times when we would laugh and watch movies together.

"What do you want to talk about?" I asked.

"I know how much I hurt you and I wish that I could take it all back but there are things that I want you to know. Things that might make it easier for you to forgive me one day. I never wanted to get married, I was practically forced into it by my parents because my Dad and her Dad are business partners. They even bought the damn ring. I'm not using it as an excuse but I was under a lot of pressure. You might not choose to believe me when I say this but I have never been in love with her. I only ever saw her as a friend and we were never...intimate. I didn't even speak to her once from the day I met you until the day I rang her to call the whole thing off."

Lukas stopped talking when Isaac entered the room, fully clothed this time. He leant against the wall with his arms crossed and looked at me, "Are you okay?"

I nodded before turning back to Lukas.

"Can we have some privacy?" he asked Isaac.

"No."

Lukas shook his head and turned back to me, "I don't want to lose you April, I need you in my life. I know it will take time but I'm willing to wait. I never thought that I could be in love with somebody who was also my best friend but you proved me wrong. I care about you and I don't want to see you get hurt again." He looked at Isaac.

"*Again* being the operative word" Isaac snapped back.

My heart was beating really fast, "Why did you go to Paris?" I asked.

"Madeline, my ex, has an internship over there. I flew over to see her because she didn't take me seriously on the phone. I needed to show her how serious I was and give her some sort of closure. Even though she took it badly, at least I've finally been honest with her and now she can move on."

"Why were you gone for a week?"

"I was only in Paris for a day but I went to Scotland straight after to see my parents. I told them that I was sick of being their puppet. My Dad got really angry and said that he never wanted to see me again but I think my Mum was secretly pleased that I'd found a girl that I was crazy about. I stayed at my best friend's house for the rest of the time and left this afternoon. I needed some time away and wanted to give you some space. I thought that was what you wanted when you didn't answer your phone or reply to my emails."

I nodded but it took me a moment to realise what he had just said, "Wait, what emails?"

"I emailed you every single day."

I thought back to when I checked my emails yesterday but I definitely didn't have any from him. But why would he lie about it? My brain was being bulldozed with information.

"Why didn't you tell me about her before we started dating?"

"If I could go back in time then I would. When I first met you, I didn't want to tell you because I was ashamed. I didn't want you to know that I was engaged to somebody who I didn't even have feelings for...it's embarrassing. I thought that you would act differently around me. By the time we started dating, I thought that if I told you then, you would wonder why I hadn't told you sooner so I kept quiet. I know it was wrong of me but when I was around you, she didn't exist. It was just me and you. But then when we took things further, I hated myself for being so selfish. I needed to tell you. Do you think that you will ever be able to forgive me?"

I could hear Isaac breathing heavily.

"I need some time to think" I replied.

"Take as much time as you need, I'll wait for you."

"I think we've heard enough" Isaac growled.

"Okay then, now it's your turn to talk, how could you do this to her?" Lukas asked.

"Do what? Make her happy?"

"Take advantage of her."

I saw Isaac's hands clench into fists as he took a step towards Lukas, "I would never take advantage of her."

Lukas stood up, "But you already have. She's your student who's been going through a tough time. Where does it say in your contract that you're allowed to sleep with your students to make them feel better?"

"You need to shut the fuck up before I make you."

"So you threaten students as well as sleeping with them?"

"I think you need to leave right now" Isaac growled.

"I think you need to find a new job" he replied.

"What's that supposed to mean?"

"You know exactly what it means. Do you really think that they're going to let you keep your job when they find out what you've done?"

"So now you're threatening to tell the university?" Isaac asked him.

"It's not a threat."

"Just think about what you're saying, you'll get April into trouble too."

"I don't need to bring her name into it."

"Will you two just shut up?" I shouted before placing my head in my hands. My head was spinning and I couldn't think straight so it didn't help that Isaac and Lukas were about to start fighting. I felt a hand on my shoulder but shrugged it off. When I looked up, I saw the hurt in Isaac's eyes.

I turned to face Lukas, "Lukas, if you care about me as much as you say you do then you won't tell anybody about me and Isaac, especially not the university."

"But..."

"No buts" I interrupted, "You need to take my word for it. I want to be able to trust you again, this is your opportunity to prove to me that I can."

After a long moment, he spoke, "Fine, I won't tell anyone but I'm doing it for you, not him."

"Thank you. I need some time to think about what you've told me tonight." I stood up, "Come on, let me walk you out."

He nodded and followed me.

"Did he pressure you?"

"No, not at all. Look, I'll explain everything to you when I'm ready but now's not the time."

"I just want you to be happy."

I nodded and watched him walk away before closing the door. Isaac came up behind me and wrapped his arms around me. When I didn't respond, he turned me around to face him.

"Hey, are you okay?"

I took a deep breath, "Why can't my life be simple?"

"It can be."

"How?" I asked, doubtful.

"I'll hand my resignation in tomorrow, simple."

My eyes widened.

"I won't lose you, April."

He pulled me into his arms and I bit my lip to stop myself from crying.

"Do you want me to stay tonight?"

I shook my head, "I need some time alone."

"I understand, do you want me to come by tomorrow?"

"Can I just ring you when I'm ready?"

"Of course." I recognised the fear in his eyes and knew that he was trying to put on a brave face for my sake.

He kissed me on my forehead before leaving. I locked the door behind him, turned the lights off and went straight to bed. Just when I thought the roller coaster was coming to a stop, it takes off again at full speed.

I always knew that I would have to see Lukas again but I hadn't expected him to just turn up on my doorstep. I also wasn't prepared for what he had to say. Although he still should have told me that he was engaged from the start, I understood why he hadn't. It reminded me of something that Katie had said about not wearing her wedding ring. He had wanted people to get to know the real him and not judge him on poor decisions that he had made in his past. It was going to take some time but I could see myself forgiving him.

I believed him when he said that he wouldn't tell anybody about me and Isaac but it got me wondering what might have happened if it was somebody else who saw us. The past couple of days with Isaac had been like a dream but what if that's all it ever was? Could it become my reality? Did I even want him to hand his resignation in when he was surrounded by memories of his sister?

I had a decision to make. A decision which would affect the rest of my life. A decision which would break somebody's heart.

Chapter Twenty Six

The next day, I could hardly keep my eyes open after only having four hours sleep. I went through three cups of coffee and a can of Red Bull but it still didn't stop me from yawning every two minutes.

At least it was Wednesday, which meant that I didn't share any classes with Lukas today. My head was still cloudy and I wasn't ready to talk to him yet.

When I had my two hour break in the afternoon, I went and hid in the library to avoid bumping into him. I considered going home but I knew that if I did that, I wouldn't go back in for my last seminar of the day.

When I got to the library, I lazily walked up and down the book aisles before I remembered what Lukas had said yesterday about sending me emails. I found a computer and logged onto my emails but there was still nothing. I even checked every single folder but they were nowhere to be found.

I walked over to the help desk and waited for the I.T guy to drag his eyes away from his computer screen. When I got tired of waiting, after about ten seconds, I rang the bell.

He looked up at me like I was a naughty child and I put on my best fake smile, "Hi, I'm wondering if you could help me? There's a problem with my emails, or rather, lack of them. I'm not receiving any."

"What's your name?" he asked in the most bored tone imaginable.

"Wow, you really love your job, huh?"

"What's your name?" he asked again.

"April Adams."

He typed my name into his computer, waited for a moment and then looked back up at me, "There's been a problem with your account."

No shit, Sherlock.

"Yes I know, that's why I'm here."

"It says that we rang you last Monday to warn you that you may experience some problems."

"Nobody rang me."

"It says my colleague Ethan spoke to you."

"Well somebody's lying because..." I closed my eyes as the memory suddenly came back to me. It was the morning that I spilt coffee all over me. "Damn."

"Do you remember now?"

"Yeah sorry, is there any way of retrieving the emails?"

"I'm working through a huge backlog, it could take another week."

"I can't wait a week. It's okay, I'll just sit here with you and wait."

He looked at me like I was crazy, "Until next week?"

I shrugged, "Do you want to play a game? I spy?"

He sighed, "Will you leave me alone if I try to retrieve yours now?"

I grinned, "Yes."

After what seemed like an eternity, he looked up at me and nodded, "Your inbox is now full."

"Thanks" I shouted over my shoulder, already on my way back to the computers.

I sat down and scrolled through the emails in my inbox wondering whether this would make things clearer for me. There were seven emails from Lukas and one from Isaac.

Half an hour later, I logged off the computer and left the library. After reading and re-reading all of the emails, I finally knew what I was going to do.

After my last seminar had finished, I went straight home for a shower and to change my clothes. Although I wasn't looking forward to hurting somebody, I knew that I was doing the right thing. I grabbed my phone and keys before heading out.

Fifteen minutes later, I arrived at Sienna's. I dialled Isaac's number and crossed my fingers that he was at home. I needed to do this.

He answered immediately, "April?"

"Are you at home?"

"Yes, why? Are you okay?"

"I'm outside, around the back."

"Wait there, I'll come down."

When he opened the door less than a minute later, I couldn't help but notice how tired and anxious he looked.

"Can we talk?" I asked.

"Of course, come in." He shut the door behind me before leading me upstairs.

As soon as we got inside his apartment, I couldn't wait any longer. I flung myself at him and buried my face in his chest, inhaling his delicious scent. He held me tight and stroked my hair. When I pulled away, I watched his face visibly relax. He led me over to the sofa and began to draw little circles in my palm, "Have you had enough time to think about what you want?"

I nodded, "Isaac...I want *you*. I've always wanted *you*."

His eyes lit up, "Are you sure? Completely sure?"

"I am 100% sure. I am head over heels in love with you."

He looked at me with so much love that there was no doubt in my mind that he felt the same way.

"I've waited such a long time to hear you say those words. I've been in love with you since the first time I met you. You're it, you're the one."

My heart felt like it was going to explode as I burst out crying.

He laughed, "Hey, what's with the April showers?"

I half giggled, half sniffed as he wiped my cheeks with his thumb. "These are happy tears" I whispered.

He grinned, "No rain, no rainbow."

I grinned back at him and then kissed him with everything that I had. It was probably really wet and sloppy from crying but I didn't care. I loved this man with every part of my being. Everything had become crystal clear after reading the emails earlier. The way that my heart had sped up when I saw Isaac's name in my inbox said it all. That one email from Isaac checking that I was okay meant more to me than all seven of Lukas's combined. I was finally following my heart like I should have done from the start.

"I handed my resignation in today" he announced as I tried to catch my breath.

"You didn't have to do that."

"I didn't have to but I wanted to. I want to be with you more than I've wanted anything in my entire life. I want to be able to hold your hand whilst we walk down the street, I want to introduce you as my girlfriend at charity events, I want to shout from the rooftops that you're mine."

I was beaming, I had never felt so happy in my whole life. I knew that it wasn't going to be plain sailing but he was worth it.

My phone began to vibrate against my leg but I ignored it.

"So what happens now?" I asked him.

"Well I had to give a month's notice so we'll have to be careful for these next few weeks but after that, the whole world is going to know that you are my girl. Forever."

"Forever" I said in agreement just as my phone started to ring again.

Damn timing.

"I'll turn it off" I said as I dug it out of my pocket. I sighed when I saw that it was Lukas. I wasn't looking forward to hurting him but I hoped that we could be friends again one day. I would be forever grateful that he was willing to keep my relationship with Isaac a secret. I was about to turn my phone off when I saw a text message scrolling across my screen -

"This is urgent. Please pick up!"

What could be urgent? I was confused because last night he had agreed to give me some time. A new message came through but this time it was a voicemail.

"I think that I should listen to this" I told Isaac. He nodded and kissed me on the head. I smiled but it quickly vanished when I heard Lukas panicking -

"April, are you there? Please pick up, I'm really worried. I've just heard, I'm on my way round now, I'll be there in a minute."

My heart was pounding. Isaac must have been able to tell that something was wrong, "What's up?" he asked.

"I don't know. It was Lukas, he sounded really worried and said that he was on his way round."

Isaac looked confused, "Round where?"

"I don't know, he wasn't making sense."

"Come on, I'll drive you home and see if he's there. If not, we can drive to his house too and check that he's okay."

I nodded as we made our way out of his apartment and down to the car park.

My mind was working overtime on the way over. Lukas was always laid back so hearing him sound so panicked made me sick with worry. I rang him back for the fourth time but it kept going straight to voicemail.

"April, it's going to be okay" Isaac tried to reassure me. I wanted to believe him but something didn't feel right. We drove the rest of the way in silence.

When we turned onto my street, my heart stopped when I saw all of the flashing lights. There were fire engines, ambulances and police cars, not to mention the crowds of people. Isaac stopped the car in front of the road block. Before I even had time to think, I got out and ran towards my house. I pushed my way through the crowds of people and went into complete shock when I saw the flames and thick black smoke billowing out of the windows.

My house was on fire.

I will never forget the smell of burning and the way the acrid smoke caught in my throat.

Two police officers were ordering the crowds to get back but I carried on pushing forward. "That's my house" I shouted to one of them. I felt a hand on my shoulder and went to shrug it off until I saw that it was Isaac, "My house...it's destroyed." He pulled me into his arms and I broke down, huge sobs racking my body.

"Miss, have you got any identification?" One of the officers asked.

I shook my head and Isaac answered for me, "Everything's in the house."

"What's your name, Miss?"

I turned to look at him, "April Adams."

"And who else lives with you?"

My whole body got chills, "Nobody, I live alone."

"Well somebody else is in the house. The fire fighters are trying to get to them now."

My knees gave way but Isaac caught me. I looked up at him and I knew that he had figured it out too.

The panicked voicemail...

Isaac's face turned white as I let out a blood curdling scream.

Lukas was in there.

To be continued...

Printed in Great Britain
by Amazon